Over the Edge

I'd just touched the steering wheel to zigzag around a rock in the path. The trouble was, it had zigged all right—but it hadn't zagged. Even when I grabbed the wheel with both hands and hauled on it, the UTV kept going in the same direction—straight toward a huge, sunken half-pipe off to the left!

"Joe! What are you doing?" Frank was holding on with both hands now as the UTV careened toward the edge of the concrete half-pipe. "Stop!"

"I'm trying!" I stomped on the brakes again and again. But it was no use. They were dead—just like the steering. There was no way to stop our vehicle from plunging over the edge to the concrete at least twenty feet below!

THE HARDY BOYS

Undercover Brothers®

Available from Simon & Schuster

HARDY BOYS

Undercover Brothers™

BOYS

FRANKLIN W. DIXON

#28 Galaxy X

Aladdin Paperbacks

New York London Toronto Sydney

This book is a work of fiction. Any references to historical events, real people, or real locales are used fictitiously. Other names, characters, places, and incidents are the product of the author's imagination, and any resemblance to actual events or locales or persons, living or dead, is entirely coincidental.

ALADDIN PAPERBACKS
An imprint of Simon & Schuster Children's Publishing Division
1230 Avenue of the Americas, New York, NY 10020
Copyright © 2009 by Simon & Schuster, Inc.
All rights reserved, including the right of reproduction in whole or in part in any form.
THE HARDY BOYS MYSTERY STORIES is a trademark of Simon & Schuster, Inc.
ALADDIN PAPERBACKS, HARDY BOYS UNDERCOVER BROTHERS, and related logos are registered trademarks of Simon & Schuster, Inc.
Designed by Sammy Yuen Jr.
The text of this book was set in Aldine 401 BT.
Manufactured in the United States of America
First Aladdin Paperbacks edition May 2009
10 9 8 7 6 5 4 3 2 1
Library of Congress Control Number 2008939521
ISBN: 978-1-4169-7801-5

TABLE OF CONTENTS

JOE

1

Dancing with Death

I never thought I'd die at the ballet.

Yeah, I admit it. That was the thought running through my head when I found myself strangling to death thirty feet off the stage. A bunch of tutu'd ballerinas were directly below me. I hoped I wouldn't take any of them out when I went *SPLAT*.

I struggled to free myself, my legs flailing around like a windmill. But it was no use. My arms were tied together in front of me with electric cords. My head and neck were squeezed between the rock-hard thighs of whatever you call the male version of a ballerina. Ballerino? Ballet dude?

The lack of oxygen was making me giddy. Or

1

maybe it was the music. A dress rehearsal was going on below me. *Swan Lake*. Until my brother Frank and I came to the ballet school, I'd never heard of it. Now I could hum it in my sleep.

I twisted my shoulders, trying again to jerk myself free. Falling thirty feet and breaking a bunch of bones didn't seem like much fun. But it was better than strangling to death.

"Quit it," the balletic baddie growled. "Trust me, you're making this harder than it needs to be."

Easy for him to say. Little sparks of light were popping in front of my eyes. The cables and lights above the stage swam giddily in front of me. I gave another weak kick. I knew I should be fighting harder, but my body was starting to feel rubbery and numb.

My eyes fluttered shut. It was too much effort to keep them open. The popping sparks got brighter. I only hoped Frank would catch my killer and make him pay. Fleecing a bunch of eager young wannabe ballerinas out of their money was bad enough. But murder . . .

"Ai-yiiiii!" A shout came from somewhere close by.

My eyes flew open—just in time to see Frank making like Tarzan, swinging in on the rope from the stage curtain!

"Oof!" the bad guy grunted as Frank's boots

connected with his midsection. Ballet Boy flew backward, tumbling off the beam where he'd been sitting while he strangled me.

That released my neck. I felt myself start to fall too. Another rope swung past me, and I automatically reached out and grabbed it. Ow. I'd almost forgotten my arms were tied. They broke loose as I grabbed on, but the cords took, like, half the skin off my wrists and hands.

"Joe!" Frank shouted as I hung there, too beat to do more than hold on. "Are you okay?"

I looked over. He'd swung onto another beam.

Then I looked down. My would-be killer was lying on the stage surrounded by shrieking ballerinas. One of his legs was twisted at a pretty funky angle. I guessed it was going to be tough to keep up those muscles in traction.

That thought gave me the strength to start climbing. "I'm cool," I told Frank hoarsely. "And I think we're done here. Time to pirouette on home—another case closed."

"I still don't see why they couldn't find any female agents to deal with that stupid ballet case," I complained.

Frank reached up to adjust his shades, then turned his head to look at me. We were lying on a couple of lounge chairs at the Bayport Community Pool. It was a hot summer day and the place was packed. But we'd found a private spot off behind the deep end where we could discuss our latest case without anyone overhearing. We'd arrived home the night before too tired to do more than fall into bed.

"I already told you, Joe," Frank said. "They couldn't find a female ATAC agent who could do the ballet thing well enough to pass for a serious student. That's why they decided to go another way and send us."

ATAC stands for American Teens Against Crime. Our father, Fenton Hardy, started it after retiring from the NYPD. It recruits teenage agents to go undercover in places where an adult investigator would have trouble blending in. Frank and I didn't have to be recruited—we signed on as soon as Dad told us about it.

The problem is, we have to keep our work with ATAC totally on the down-low. Nobody's allowed to know what we do. Not even the rest of the family. That causes some complications, especially when Mom and Aunt Trudy start asking questions. But the rewards of the ATAC gig definitely make up for its drawbacks.

Well, most of the time, anyway. "It's bad enough

we had to deal with all that ballet," I grumbled, not quite ready to let it go. "But then you get the sweet deal of playing personal trainer, and I'm stuck pretending to be a janitor!"

Frank shrugged. "Not my call, bro. I was just playing the role I was assigned."

"Whatever." I rubbed my sore neck. "I just hope our next mission isn't going undercover as a couple of shampoo boys at some beauty school."

Frank grinned. "No way. They'll probably send us to a Mr. Nice Guyz concert disguised as presidents of their fan club."

"Dude, don't even joke about that!" I was actually sort of impressed that Frank knew who Mr. Nice Guyz was. He doesn't exactly keep up with all the latest bands. Not that I kept up much with that particular one myself—I'm not really into blow-dried boy bands. "No, I've got it," I went on. "We'll probably have to investigate some wrongdoing at the next big shoe sale at the mall."

Frank chuckled. "Hey, it's just part of the deal," he reminded me. "We go where they need us, right?"

"Yeah, yeah," I said. "I just wish they needed us in, say, Hawaii. Or maybe a surfing convention in Jamaica." I squinted around at the crowded scene surrounding us. "Unfortunately, it's looking like we'll have to settle for this place and our boring backyard for the rest of summer vacation."

Frank didn't answer. He was staring at something out in the pool.

Following his gaze, I saw that he wasn't watching some*thing* after all. He was watching some*one*. A girl around our age. She didn't look like much of a swimmer—she was sort of thrashing around out there—but from what I could see, she looked superhot. Once again, I was sort of impressed. Frank isn't exactly Mr. Smooth when it comes to the ladies. Actually, he has this annoying habit of not even noticing them much of the time. Okay, that's not the annoying part. The annoying part is that *they* usually notice *him*. I guess a lot of girls out there go for the strong, silent, nerdy type.

Frank stood up. "Where are you going?" I asked, jumping to my feet as well. I wasn't about to let him beat me to a hottie!

"It looks like she's having some trouble," he said.

Before I could answer, the girl started thrashing around more violently than ever. "Help!" she shrieked. "I'm drowning!"

Dive In

"**H**ang on!" I shouted.

Acting on instinct, I raced to the edge of the pool and dove in. Luckily, the girl was only a few yards from the edge of the pool where Joe and I had been sitting. I reached her in about three strokes.

She stopped thrashing when I got there. I grabbed her under the arms, making sure her head stayed above water.

"Just relax," I said. "I've got you."

She sort of gurgled and nodded. Her body relaxed, allowing me to drag her along with me.

I turned and struck out for dry land, holding on to the girl with one arm and swimming with the other. By the time we reached the edge of the pool, a small crowd had gathered.

"It's okay," Joe was saying to the onlookers. "My brother is trained in water rescue."

That was true. Both of us had taken a course when we'd signed on with ATAC. We'd also learned a bunch of other cool stuff, from rappelling to judo.

"Hey, what's going on?" The lifeguard on duty pushed his way forward.

I grimaced. Said lifeguard was Brian Conrad. He's this guy we know from school. I'd been a little surprised to show up at the pool and see that he'd landed a job as lifeguard. He normally isn't the helping-people type. Or the holding-down-a-job type, for that matter.

"Can you grab the edge?" I asked the girl, ignoring Brian.

She nodded and reached for the edge of the pool. "Thanks, I'm okay now," she said. "I can get out myself."

"No, hang on, I'll help you." Joe was already reaching for her hands.

"Hey, back off, amateurs." Brian had reached us. "Pulling people out of the pool is my job."

Joe shot him a look. "If we had to wait for you to actually do *your* job, she'd be at the bottom of the pool right now."

"Whatever. Come on, babe." Brian reached for the girl.

She shook off his hand. "I'm fine," she said coolly, hoisting herself out of the pool in one graceful motion.

She was amazing-looking. I tried not to stare.

Joe wasn't even trying. His eyes were practically bulging out of his head.

The girl turned to me, still ignoring Brian. "Thank you so much for coming to my rescue," she said, putting a hand on my arm.

"That's my brother." Joe shouldered past Brian to get closer to the girl. "He's a real hero. We have a lot in common that way. How about if you sit down and catch your breath, and I'll tell you all about it?"

"Forget it, Joe Hardhead," Brian said. "This girl needs medical attention. I'll take over from here."

The girl gave him an icy look. "I already said I'm fine. I don't need a doctor."

Before Brian could respond, she took me by the arm and dragged me after her. Joe followed. Most of the other onlookers drifted away, the excitement over.

I glanced back over my shoulder at Brian. He was sort of gritting his teeth. He took a few steps after us. But just then a big, beefy-looking guy in his twenties appeared. He was wearing swim trunks and a whistle.

"Yo, Conrad," he barked. "Why aren't you at your post?" He pointed to the empty lifeguard stand.

Joe snorted with laughter as Brian started to whine excuses at his boss. "Nice," he commented. "Wonder how long Brian's going to last at this job?"

The girl didn't seem interested in any of that. She dropped my arm as we reached a lounge chair with a flowered bag on it. Reaching into the bag, she pulled out a large hardcover book.

"I wish I had something better to give you to show my thanks. But this will have to do." With that, she shoved the book into my hands.

I glanced down at it. It looked like some kind of sweeping historical novel. Not really my thing—not that I was about to tell her that.

"Um, thanks," I said. "But it was really no big . . ."

My voice trailed off. She'd just grabbed the bag off the chair and rushed away. "Be sure to read that book, okay?" she called back over her shoulder. "Do it for me!"

"Hey!" Joe called after her. "Come back. You didn't even tell us your name."

"Give it up, Joe," I said as the girl disappeared around the corner. "If you wanted her number, you missed your chance."

He frowned. "Maybe her name and number are written inside the book," he suggested. "She seemed pretty eager for you to read it."

The guy never gives up hope. Mostly just to appease him, I flipped open the cover. My eyes widened immediately, and I slammed the book shut again.

"What?" Joe asked.

I tucked the book carefully under my arm. "Come on," I told him. "I think we'd better head home."

"As soon as I opened that book and saw the DVD stuck inside, I figured we'd just received our next mission," I commented as I sat down in front of the video game console on my desk.

Joe and I were in my bedroom at home. We'd rushed back from the pool to find the house empty. Aunt Trudy was weeding the flower garden out back, but we'd sneaked past without letting her know we were home. Sometimes that was easier than answering her questions. Okay, make that *most* of the time.

Joe shook his head as he flopped onto the end

of my bed. "I can't believe that girl was an ATAC agent," he said. "Dude, why can't *she* be my partner instead of you?"

Ignoring him, I slid the DVD out of the book. The label made it look like a concert video from the latest Mr. Nice Guyz tour. All our ATAC assignments come on CDs or DVDs. One play is all we get to take in the details of our next assignment. After that, they revert to whatever's on the label—movie, music, video game, whatever. So it's key to pay attention the first time.

Paying attention isn't always Joe's strong suit, so I glanced back at him. "Ready?" I asked, my finger poised over the start button.

"Let's do it." He sat up and leaned forward. "And let's hope that it isn't another girly assignment."

The DVD began with the usual welcome from our ATAC boss, who went by the name Q. After that, the briefing started.

"Welcome to a whole new galaxy of action and excitement," a voice intoned to a background of wailing guitar-heavy music. The picture on the screen jumped to a shot of a hilly, brushy outdoor track of some sort. Several mountain bikes raced past, jumping and skidding along the track. Then the shot jumped to a steep, icy mountain, with several skiers whooshing past at top speed. After that, the

scene shifted again, this time to crashing waves with surfers riding in on longboards.

"Awesome!" Joe blurted out, his eyes glued to the screen.

"Still worried it's going to be a girly assignment?" I joked.

Then I shut up, because the voice was speaking again. *"Welcome to Galaxy X,"* it said. *"A brand-new theme park certain to be a dream destination for anyone who craves some radical excitement in their lives."*

"Whoa, Galaxy X? I've heard about that place," Joe said. "It's being built on some island off the Carolina coast, right?"

I nodded. "I've heard of it too. It's supposed to be the brainchild of Tyrone McKenzie."

"The music producer?"

"Uh-huh." I'd just read a story about McKenzie and his pet project in a news magazine. Hitting pause, I searched my mind for the details. "The place is supposed to be a dream come true for teenage boys. There are regular theme-park-type attractions like roller coasters and stuff, but it goes way beyond that."

"I know!" Joe put in. "I saw a whole story about it on TV last week. There's going to be a huge BMX track, rock-climbing walls, a totally cool skateboard park, a wave pool, cliff diving, street luge, snowboarding . . ."

"Sounds like fun." I pressed the button to start the recording again.

The announcer told us pretty much everything we'd just discussed. Basically, Galaxy X was going to be a testosterone paradise. In addition to the X Game–type stuff and the roller coasters, there would be a huge arcade, tons of food, awesome 3-D movies, and lots more.

"Sounds like fun, right?" the voice on the DVD said. *"Well, apparently somebody doesn't think so. Tyrone McKenzie has been receiving threats from someone who doesn't want Galaxy X to open at all. When these threats were limited to e-mail and blogs, Mr. McKenzie wasn't concerned. However, recently there has been some graffiti and other vandalism at the site itself, and with the grand opening approaching, he called the authorities. And that's where you come in. . . ."*

"Yes!" Joe jumped to his feet and pumped both fists in the air. "Galaxy X, here we come!"

"Hang on," I cautioned him. "We don't want to miss the rest of the message."

But there wasn't much after that. The announcer explained that Joe and I would be heading down to Galaxy X immediately, arriving just before the start of something Tyrone McKenzie was calling "Preview Daze." That was when the park would be open only to various young, hip celebrities, reviewers, and other media types. Joe and I would be posing as radio contest winners who'd scored tickets to the preview. We were supposed to blend in and investigate—find out if there was any real danger behind the threats.

Finally, Q reappeared onscreen. *"Be careful, agents,"* he warned in his usual super-serious way. Then he shot the camera a quick "hang loose" sign with one hand and cracked a smile. *"And have fun."*

With that, the screen went black. "Wow, this is great," Joe said, hopping around the room like the ball in a pinball machine. "This has to be the greatest mission ever!"

"Not exactly," I said. "Based on what we just heard, we don't even know what we're supposed to be looking for."

Joe shrugged. "So what? That's nothing new—our missions are usually mysterious like that. Look at the big picture, man. Even if this McKenzie dude is being totally paranoid and it's just a few disgruntled bloggers behind the trouble, we still end up with a few free days of hanging out with celebs and having an awesome time testing out all those cool attractions before the place even opens to the public." He grinned and lifted one hand. "And here we thought we'd be stuck here and bored for the rest of our summer vacation!"

I couldn't help grinning back and giving him a high five. "Okay, maybe you're right," I admitted. "It definitely beats ballet."

X Marks the Spot

"**A**wesome!" I cried as the chopper banked for a turn, swooping down and skimming along the coast. We were so low I could see the waves breaking on the rocky shoreline.

Frank and I were in Tyrone McKenzie's private helicopter, flying over the barrier islands off the coast of North Carolina. Our pilot was a young ex-military guy with a buzz cut and a fun-loving attitude. As soon as he'd realized we were game for some fun, he'd started showing off his skills. We hadn't even arrived at Galaxy X yet, and this mission was already a blast!

"Check it out," Frank said from the seat beside me. "I found another interesting site. Looks like those bloggers the ATAC material mentioned are ramping up their attacks now that the park is about to open."

I tore my gaze away from the view long enough to glance over. Frank was hunched over his laptop. Well, as hunched as he could get with his safety belt and shoulder strap firmly and properly attached, that is. Typical Frank.

"You're missing some great scenery," I told him. "Not to mention an amazing ride." I leaned forward and clapped the pilot on the shoulder. He glanced back and gave me a grin and a thumbs-up.

"Never mind that." Frank looked up. After shooting a glance at the pilot to make sure he wasn't listening, he went on. "Look at this—there's a guy out there posting all over the web, claiming he'll do anything he can to stop Galaxy X from becoming a success."

I sighed. Frank could be a nerd sometimes, but he was a persistent nerd. I figured I'd better look at what he'd found. Then maybe he'd leave me alone and I could go back to enjoying the ride.

"Who is he?" I asked, leaning over for a look at the screen.

It was a skateboarding message board. Frank pointed to a post at the top. The headline read REAL SK8RS UNITE! and the poster's tag was Sk8rH8r.

"Skater Hater," I said. "Clever. So what's he ranting about?"

Frank scrolled farther down. "He says GX will just be a way for coddled suburban kids to pretend they're living on the edge," he said. "He seems to think it will cheapen the experience of real X Gamer types."

"I see his point, I guess." I shrugged. "Doesn't seem worth getting so worked up about, though. It'd be like us freaking out over kids pretending to ride motorcycles in video games just because we ride ours for real. I mean, who cares?"

"A lot of people, apparently." Frank clicked on a different tab so a new site displayed. STOP GX! was at the top in huge, blinking neon letters.

"Whoa." I grabbed the laptop and scrolled down, scanning the site. It seemed people really were angry about this theme park. Angry enough to create a whole website about it. "But like I said, who cares? If the park is as lame as they all claim, it'll fail anyway."

"Doubtful. Just about everything Tyrone McKenzie touches turns to gold." Frank leaned over and clicked onto a new site, this one a biography of the wealthy music producer. "See?"

"I'll take your word for it." I handed back the laptop. We would be at Galaxy X soon, and I didn't want to waste any more of the flight on boring research. I figured we'd get a feel for what was going on when we arrived.

Frank frowned. "Look, don't forget this is a mission, not a vacation," he said in his nerdiest older-brother voice. "We need to be up to speed when we get there. Preview Daze starts tomorrow, remember?"

"What's to research? You already dug up those anti-GX websites—what else is there to know?" I was feeling kind of impatient. The pilot had settled down and was flying straight. I really wanted to encourage him to throw in a few more stunts before we reached our destination. But I couldn't with Frank buzzing in my ear.

"Well, for one thing, it would help to get familiar with McKenzie's background and family situation." Now Frank was morphing from dorky older brother to stodgy professor. "It always helps to be prepared."

"Thanks, Scout Leader Hardy." I rolled my eyes off Frank's disapproving look. "Whatever. Why don't you fill me in on the gist?"

"Fine. McKenzie himself is a media mogul—he produces not only tons of music acts, but some TV and other stuff as well." Frank scanned the page in front of him. "It says here he's an avid amateur astronomer, loves all sports, and was a competitive skier for a while when he was younger. Opening a place like Galaxy X, aimed at what he calls 'boys and boys at heart,' is a lifelong dream."

I snorted. "Boys at heart?"

Even Frank grinned and shook his head. "Anyway, he has one kid from his first marriage—a son, Nicholas, who's a few years older than us. Then there's an eighteen-year-old stepdaughter from his second marriage. Then, from his third marriage—"

"Whoa, how many times has this dude gotten hitched?"

Frank shot me a look. I could practically read the thought balloon: *If you'd done any research you'd already know that, you hopeless slacker.*

But he didn't say it. "Three, actually," he said instead. "His current wife is a former beauty queen from Texas. They have an infant son named Tyrone Jr."

At that moment the chopper banked sharply, tossing us both against our safety belts. The pilot pulled off his earphones and glanced back. "Sorry about that, guys," he yelled over the roar of the engine. "Just avoiding a bird. We'll be arriving at Galaxy X soon."

"Thanks!" I leaned over and pressed my face

against the window, scanning the horizon for the first glimpse of GX.

"You heard him, Joe. We don't have much time to review this stuff, so . . . ," Frank said.

"Right," I agreed. "That means it's too late. We might as well forget the homework and play it by ear for now."

Frank frowned. He hates when I want to play things by ear.

"Okay, even if you don't care about the background info, maybe you'll be interested in the list of celebrities who are supposed to turn up to this preview thing." He tapped another few keys, then turned the screen toward me. "Here it is."

That piqued my curiosity a little. Leaning toward him again, I scanned the list. It consisted mostly of rock stars, professional athletes, and well-known young actors. I also spotted a sportscaster, some TV hosts, and a couple of comedians. Several hot bands were scheduled to perform at the grand opening, including Mr. Nice Guyz, the Royal We, and other familiar names from the top of the charts.

"Whoa, check it out!" I exclaimed. "Cody Zane and David Sanders are coming."

"Who?" said Frank. "Oh, wait. You mean those skateboard guys?"

"Not just *those* skateboard guys," I said. "*The*

skateboard guys. They're incredible! I swear, some of their moves totally defy gravity."

Frank tapped more keys. "Hmm, looks like Cody Zane is playing a major role this week, actually," he said with interest. "There's going to be some kind of contest. . . ."

I wasn't really listening after that. That was because I'd just leaned back to the window and caught my first glimpse of Galaxy X.

And trust me, there was no mistaking it. I mean, where else would you see a five-hundred-foot-tall volcano rising up out of the otherwise flat chain of barrier islands?

Even Frank lost interest in his research when I pointed it out. And no wonder. The closer we got, the more spectacular GX looked.

For one thing, the place was huge. In addition to the enormous fake mountain at the center, there was tons of gleaming metal everywhere—roller coaster tracks, a bunch of parked vehicles that looked like Indy cars, and more that I couldn't make out from the air. I spotted several big domes, like the kind you see over indoor tennis courts. There were some long dirt tracks that I guessed were for BMX or similar sports. Swathes of sparkling white snow coated the northern slopes of the mountain. A space shuttle—yeah, that's right, a freaking full-size *space shuttle*—was parked near the base of the ski slopes. Even in the bright daylight, neon was visible all over the place. And water was everywhere—surrounding most of the base of the mountain and in large pools throughout the park.

"The whole place is laid out in the shape of a big X," Frank commented as he peered down through his own window.

"Hey, you're right!" I hadn't noticed until he said it. But the two main paths through the park did form a huge X. They seemed to be paved with something different from the rest—black asphalt inset with silvery metallic stuff that glinted brightly in the sunlight.

"Landing in five, guys!" the pilot called back to us as the chopper swooped lower.

I saw that we were aiming for a cluster of nondescript buildings at one edge of the big X. We landed on the roof of the largest one, a sleek, low-slung, office-type building.

"Welcome to GX HQ," the pilot said, saluting. "Enjoy your stay at the coolest place in the galaxy."

It sounded pretty scripted. But who cared? I couldn't wait to get out and start checking out the place!

Soon we were standing in a hushed, overly

air-conditioned office lobby. Expensive-looking oil paintings hung on the walls, and everything seemed to be made of mahogany and brass.

"I'm so sorry," the receptionist told us. "Mr. McKenzie was expecting you, but he got called away unexpectedly to meet with local news media at the base of Mount McKenzie."

Mount McKenzie, huh? Okay, research or no research, I already knew at least one thing about this Tyrone McKenzie guy. He definitely had a serious ego!

A man had stepped into the reception area just in time to hear what the receptionist said. "Typical," he grunted. "Tyrone never thinks twice about making everyone else wait for him."

I looked the newcomer over. He was maybe fifty years old, tall and sort of swarthy, with permanent frown lines in his brow. His suit looked like it probably cost more than my parents' house.

Meanwhile Frank was still talking to the receptionist. "Maybe we can head out and track him down," he suggested. "We're really, uh, eager to get settled in."

McKenzie himself knew we were coming, of course. So did his immediate family. But our ATAC instructions had warned us not to clue anyone else in on our true identities—not even McKenzie's employees. There was no telling whether any of them might be involved. So as far as the receptionist knew, we were just a couple of ordinary brothers who'd won a radio contest.

"I don't know . . . ," she said, sounding dubious. "Preview Daze hasn't officially started yet, which means the park is still technically closed to everyone except staff and crew. I think perhaps it would be better if you had a seat and waited for Mr. McKenzie to return."

"Why should these two young men waste a beautiful morning sitting around waiting for Tyrone to remember they exist?" The swarthy guy stepped forward and extended a hand toward us. "You two must be the contest winners I heard were coming, eh? Congratulations, and welcome to Galaxy X. I'm Jack Smith, one of Mr. McKenzie's business partners."

Frank and I shook hands and introduced ourselves. "We're really looking forward to checking this place out," I said.

Smith chuckled. "I'm sure you are. It's quite an experience." He gestured for us to follow him past the reception desk. "Come on, I'll show you how to find Tyrone."

Ignoring the receptionist, who still looked worried, Frank and I followed. We headed into a hallway and then down some stairs. Soon we were stepping outside into a small parking lot. Half a dozen shiny new Utility Terrain Vehicles were parked near the door.

"Sweet!" I exclaimed, hurrying forward to check them out.

A big, beefy young security guard stepped forward to block me. "Can I help you?" he said in a polite but firm voice. "This is a restricted area."

"It's okay, Wallace." Smith had emerged by now. "These are a couple of our radio contest winners. I was just going to point them toward Mount McKenzie so Mr. McKenzie can welcome them to Galaxy X. I was thinking they could take one of the dune buggies here."

"Oh!" Wallace's expression lightened up. He actually looked pretty friendly when he wasn't going all stern on us. "Yeah, it's a hot day and the mountain is pretty far. Why don't you borrow Nick's vehicle?" The guard waved a hand at one of the UTVs, a bright purple number with silver racing stripes. "I'm sure he wouldn't mind."

Wallace was sweating like crazy in his long-sleeved guard uniform. He also didn't look like he was in very good shape. I guessed Frank and I wouldn't have any trouble making it halfway across the park on foot without collapsing. Still, I wasn't about to turn down a chance to test-drive one of the UTVs.

"Sure!" I said before Frank could open his mouth. "Thanks, that'd be awesome."

"All right then." Smith was already turning to head back inside. "I'll let Wallace give you directions. Enjoy your stay, boys."

"Thank you, sir," Frank said. "We appreciate your help."

"I'll drive," I volunteered, vaulting into the UTV before Frank could protest. "And I don't think we need directions. I'm guessing we just aim for that." I pointed at the mountain rising from the center of the park.

Wallace looked amused. "Pretty much," he agreed. "Just take that path on the other side of the lot and make a left onto the main path. The mountain will be dead ahead."

"Thanks." Frank climbed into the passenger seat. The guard gave us a wave, then wandered back to his post near the door. He looked kind of bored. It had to be tough just to stand around doing the guard thing with all that cool stuff so close at hand.

But I forgot about Wallace as I started the UTV. "Sweet," I declared as the engine roared to life. "This thing's really souped up!"

"Just be careful," said Frank.

I grinned at him and revved the engine. He rolled his eyes, but I thought I caught a ghost of a smile. Frank might be kind of uptight sometimes, but underneath his Mr. Good Guy front he loves action and adventure as much as I do.

Aiming for the path, I stepped on the gas. The UTV handled like a dream. All I had to do was breathe on the wheel to get it weaving back and forth. Talk about power steering!

As soon as we'd rounded the corner onto one of those wide, glittery black paths we'd seen from the air, I opened her up a little. "Let's see what this baby can do!" I called over the roar of the engine. We passed the entrance to a roller coaster called the Leap and a couple of snack and souvenir stands, moving faster and faster.

"Take it easy, Joe." Frank clutched the edge of his seat as I careened around another corner onto a smaller, white-paved path past a huge sign proclaiming that this part of the park was SK8R PARADISE. "Hey, where are you going? The mountain's that way!"

"Don't worry," I yelled back. Kicking her back up to top speed, I turned back toward the main path, aiming for the mountain rising in the distance straight ahead. "Just taking a little detour. This thing can handle—whoa!"

I'd just touched the steering wheel to zigzag around a rock in the path. The trouble was, it had zigged all right—but it hadn't zagged. Even when I grabbed the wheel with both hands and hauled on it, the UTV kept going in the same direction—straight toward a huge, sunken half-pipe off to the left!

"Joe! What are you doing?" Frank was holding on with both hands now as the UTV careened toward the edge of the concrete half-pipe. "Stop!"

"I'm trying!" I stomped on the brakes again and again. But it was no use. They were dead—just like the steering. There was no way to stop our vehicle from plunging over the edge to the concrete at least twenty feet below!

No Time to Lose

"Jump!" Joe shouted.

I didn't have to be told twice. I pushed off against my seat.

"Oof!" I hit the ground hard, rolling over several times. Yeah, that was definitely going to leave a bruise.

CRASH!

I winced as I heard the UTV smash against the ground far below. Pieces clattered against the smooth sides of the half-pipe, and what looked like a piece of the bumper flew up over the edge and landed on the grass near me.

I sat up, rubbing my shoulder and elbow, and glanced around for Joe. He was just sitting up a few yards away. His face was pale.

"Whoa," he said. Pushing himself to his feet, he hurried to the edge. "Close call."

"A little too close." I joined him and looked down. The UTV was smashed to smithereens. If we'd been in it . . . "You okay?" I asked.

Joe nodded. "A few scrapes and bruises," he said. "I'll live. You?"

"Ditto." I brushed the dirt off my shorts, then squinted toward the mountain rising in the center of the park. "Looks like we'll be walking the rest of the way."

"Yeah." Joe started to turn away, then shot one last look into the half-pipe. "But on the bright side, this place rules. Check out that half-pipe! Can't wait to give it a try."

I couldn't help laughing. That's my brother for you: Mr. Short Attention Span!

It was an interesting walk to the base of Mount McKenzie. We passed all kinds of cool attractions, from an enormous neon-encrusted video arcade to a Wild West–themed building called the Saloon. I had to practically put a leash on Joe to get him past the entrance to the BMX track.

The man-made mountain looked even more impressive up close. Its southern slopes were dotted with different climbing walls and zip lines.

The snowy northern half wasn't visible from this angle.

Tyrone McKenzie was standing near the edge of the man-made lake at the base of the biggest climbing wall. I recognized him right away from my research. He was an average-looking guy of average height. Still, there was something commanding about him. Maybe it was the expensive haircut, or the carefully casual khakis and shirt, or the South Pacific tan. Then again, maybe it was the knowledge that he was worth something north of a billion bucks.

In any case, he was on his cell phone at the moment. Several people I assumed to be his family were watching the local news crew pack up its equipment. Joe and I waited until the news crew had hurried off, then stepped forward and introduced ourselves.

"Right," McKenzie said, lowering his cell phone—actually a super-high-tech PDA—from his ear. "Glad you finally made it. Are you going to help me track down whoever's trying to ruin me?"

"We're certainly going to try, sir." I glanced at the others. "Is it safe to talk freely?"

"Huh?" McKenzie had glanced down at his PDA again while I was talking. Now he looked up and around. "Oh. Of course. This is my family—my wife, Delfina, and our son, Tyrone Jr. That's Erica over there, and Nick."

"Lovely to meet you," Delfina trilled. She was tall, blond, and stunning. And pretty young-looking. The pudgy baby she was holding was playing happily with a pair of expensive-looking sunglasses.

Speaking of Nick, he barely bothered to mumble a hello before returning his attention to his iPod. He looked a lot like his father, except that he was a little shorter and had reddish hair.

Then there was Erica, McKenzie's eighteen-year-old stepdaughter. "Hi, there," she greeted me and Joe with an easy smile. "So you're the good guys riding to the rescue, huh?"

"Something like that," said Joe. It was pretty obvious he was checking her out. Not that I could blame him. Erica was really cute—sort of spunky and tomboyish, with close-cropped dark hair and intelligent eyes.

"Whatever." Nick looked up from his iPod with a frown. "Can I go now?"

McKenzie had returned his attention to his PDA. But now he focused on the rest of us again. "Stay put, sport," he ordered Nick shortly. Then he looked at me. "So what are your plans to put a stop to this mischief?"

No wonder this guy was such a success in business. He was pretty intimidating. Still, I stared right back at him.

"That depends on what you have to tell us," I said. "We know you've received threats by e-mail and phone, and that there was some sort of vandalism. . . ."

McKenzie slid his PDA into his shirt pocket. "Right. Bunch of graffiti just outside the main gate." He scowled. "Probably just the usual rabble-rousers behind that, though."

"Environmental protesters," Erica put in helpfully. "They're been picketing out there since way before this place was ready to open."

Interesting. I traded a glance with Joe.

"Can we see it?" Joe asked. "The graffiti, I mean."

"Too late," McKenzie replied. "Had it cleaned up immediately. Preview Daze starts first thing in the a.m., you know."

"Well, what did it say?" I asked.

"It was horrible," Delfina piped up, clutching baby Tyrone Jr. closer to her chest. "It said to close down, or else! Isn't that rude?"

I glanced at McKenzie. He'd just reached into his pocket and pulled out his PDA again. Based on his attitude so far, he didn't seem to be taking this too seriously.

"Listen," I said. "Joe and I just had a close call ourselves on the way over here."

"What do you mean?" Delfina's round blue eyes widened even more with concern.

Joe shrugged. "Not sure if it's connected or not," he said, "but the UTV we borrowed from your HQ lost its brakes and steering halfway here."

"Really?" McKenzie looked up. "I paid a bundle for those things—they're brand-new. Are you sure?"

"Definitely." I grimaced. "If you don't believe us, check out the half-pipe with the dragon mural behind it. The UTV is there—what's left of it, anyway. At the moment it's pretty much a shiny purple mess."

"Purple?" Nick squawked, suddenly looking more interested in our presence than he had all along. "Wait, you mean you wrecked the *purple* UTV? But that one's mine!"

"Was," Joe corrected. I could tell he was trying to hold back a laugh. "It *was* yours. Now it's the scrapyard's. Sorry, dude."

McKenzie's fingers were flying over the tiny keyboard on his PDA. "I'll text someone to get over there and clean it up," he said. "But don't read too much into one little mishap. We were down to the wire on construction thanks to the weather— in fact, three or four of the attractions still aren't finished. It probably wasn't the steering at all—you probably just hit a stray nail or something. I'll speak to the janitorial staff personally and make sure they go over things with a fine-tooth comb before the celebrities start arriving tomorrow."

"Yeah, right," Joe muttered under his breath so that only I could hear. "Like I don't know the diff between a flat tire and a complete lack of brakes and steering!"

He had a point. "Listen," I spoke up. "I really don't think it was just a nail. We really have to consider whether—"

Before I could get out the rest of my sentence, McKenzie's PDA buzzed. He stopped texting long enough to peer at the screen. Then he grumbled under his breath.

"Excuse me," he said to me and Joe distractedly. "I'd better take this—it's my insurance agent. If you have any other questions, my family will be happy to help you." With that, he pressed the PDA to his ear and hurried off.

I sighed. So far Joe and I didn't know much more than we had when we'd arrived. Well, except that the potential victim of all this was taking it about as seriously as an annoying hangnail.

Glancing around, I saw that Nick was glaring at Joe, clearly mourning the loss of his UTV. Delfina was cooing at her baby. The only one who seemed at all tuned in to things was Erica.

"Sorry about my father," she said to me with a wry smile. "He's a little obsessed with this grand opening. Not much gets through to him these days."

I chuckled. "Yeah, I can see that."

"Excuse me, boys," Delfina spoke up. "The little prince is late for his nap. I'd better head home before he gets cranky. Ta-ta!"

She toddled off on her four-inch heels, crooning to the baby as she went. "Too bad, ATAC dudes," Nick said sarcastically as soon as his stepmother was out of earshot. "Looks like you've been deprived of Delfina's wit and intellect. Now you'll never solve the case!"

"Stop it." Erica shot him a frown. "Why do you have to act like such a jerk all the time?"

"Who's acting?" Nick smirked. Then he returned to glaring at Joe. "So why'd you have to wreck my UTV, anyway?"

"Look, I'm sorry it got trashed," Joe said. "But it wasn't some conspiracy or anything, okay? It just happened to be the first one in line. Anyway, in case you missed it, I didn't exactly wreck it. The brakes and steering cut out. You're lucky it wasn't you driving at the time."

"You're sure everything cut out?" asked Erica.

"Positive," Joe replied. "Not that your father seemed to believe it."

Nick rolled his eyes. "Yeah, that's Dad for you. Just for future reference, you might want to save your breath instead of trying to argue with him. He's always right—even when he's wrong. If you catch my drift."

Meanwhile Erica was biting her lip. "Wow," she said softly. "The brakes and the steering at the same time . . . that can't have been coincidence."

"My sister, the gearhead, everyone," said Nick sarcastically.

"*Step*sister," Erica corrected. "I don't want anyone thinking I share the same DNA as you."

I barely heard their bickering. Erica was right. There was little chance the UTV's malfunctioning had been an accident. That left one question—had someone wanted to put Joe and me out of commission before we could start our investigation?

"Listen," I said. "What do you two know about this Jack Smith guy we met back at the office?"

SUSPECT PROFILE

Name: Jack Smith

Hometown: Atlanta, Georgia

Physical description: Age 53, 6'1", 195 lbs., graying brown hair, brown eyes.

Nick just shrugged. "What's to know?" he said.
"Just another stiff in a suit, like *all* of Dad's boring
business peeps."

"I don't know much about him either," Erica
said. "Why?"

Joe looked at me, clearly guessing what I was
thinking. "Oh, no reason," he said. "Except that he
was the one who suggested we take a UTV to get
over here."

"Oh!" Erica's eyes widened. "Well, like I said,
I don't know much about Mr. Smith. He's
only been Dad's business partner for maybe six
months." Glancing around, she lowered her voice.
"Although actually, now that you mention it, one

of Dad's secretaries claims he used to be a hit man for the mob." She shrugged, her voice returning to its usual volume. "Still, I doubt that's true."

I doubted it too. But you never know. I made a mental note to e-mail the research team back at ATAC as soon as I could. They could dig up the dirt on Jack Smith if anyone could.

I was jolted out of my thoughts by a sudden, loud, high-pitched scream. It came from somewhere nearby, and was followed instantly by the terrified squall of a baby!

No Guts, No Glory

"That sounded like Delfina!" Erica exclaimed. "Come on!" I raced toward the source of the scream. Frank was right at my heels, with Erica and Nick behind him.

When I skidded around the corner of a snack bar, I saw Delfina. She was sprawled on her back in the middle of the path, with baby Tyrone Jr. clutched protectively to her body.

"Stop!" she sobbed loudly when she spotted us. "Don't come any closer—black ice!"

She was right. I felt my foot start to slide. Pulling back just in time, I held out my arms to stop the others.

"Don't even try," I said. "That's some serious ice."

"Where can we get some rope?" Frank asked Nick and Erica.

"I'm on it." Erica took off for the nearest set of attractions. We were within view of the snowy northern slopes of Mount McKenzie by now—though still nowhere near close enough to explain the mysterious ice spill.

"I'd better call Dad," said Nick, pulling out a cell phone.

Soon Erica was back with a sturdy rock-climbing rope. We tossed it to Delfina and hauled her back to nonslippery ground.

"Thank you so much," Delfina gasped out as she climbed to her feet, still hugging her baby compulsively. "I was sure poor little Tyrone Jr. was going to be hurt!"

Despite her worry, Tyrone Jr. had calmed down and seemed fairly unimpressed with the whole situation. He just sucked on one fat little fist and stared at us.

"What about you? Are you okay?" I asked as Delfina tottered slightly in place.

"Oh, I'm fine." She gave a shaky laugh, then let go of the baby with one hand just long enough to reach down and pull off her stilettos. "Broke a heel, that's all."

"What's going on here?" McKenzie shouted, racing toward us.

"Stop right there, sir!" Frank hurried forward to meet him. He grabbed the man by the arm just in time to steer him around the edge of the black ice.

"What are you doing?" McKenzie snapped at him, shaking off his hand.

"Oh, it was terrible, sweetie!" Delfina cried, rushing over to him. Lucky for Frank. It looked like McKenzie was ready to strangle him with his bare hands. "I was just walking along with Tyrone Jr., and then I felt my feet go out from under me. . . ."

Soon McKenzie was up to speed. "This is an outrage!" he ranted, stomping around in a circle, glaring at the ice. Frankly, I'm surprised it didn't burn away instantly under the force of his blazing eyes. "I won't have my family endangered. Enough is enough!"

He punched in a number on his PDA. "Stella?" he barked at whoever answered. "Get me the police on the phone. No, the FBI. Both!"

I winced, wondering if he'd call in the CIA and the National Guard next. He seemed to be taking things a lot more seriously now that his wife and baby were involved. It was such a complete 180 from his previous attitude that I wasn't sure what to say for a second.

"Just calm down, sir." Frank stepped forward. His shoulders were squared, and he was wearing his best straight-A-Eagle-Scout expression. "Please don't do anything rash."

"What?" McKenzie thundered.

"Joe and I are already here ready to handle this," Frank told McKenzie, his voice calm but firm. "Flying off the handle and calling in everybody and anybody won't help. If anything, it will tip off whoever's doing this and make them more careful. If you just give us a chance to look into things, we should have a much better shot of finding the culprit."

McKenzie stared at Frank for a long moment. Nobody said a word. A glance around at the man's family members showed that they were all staring at Frank in shock. I guessed they weren't used to seeing someone stand up to McKenzie. And no wonder. He definitely seemed like a guy who was used to getting his way.

Then McKenzie . . . laughed? "Well said, son," he said, clapping Frank on the back. Then he tucked his PDA back in his pocket. "Not just everyone has the guts to stand up and speak his mind like that. Come to think of it, you remind me of myself at your age." He winked. "And you're absolutely right. I brought you boys in to do the job, and now it's time for me to get out of your way and let you get to work."

I let out a sigh of relief. For a second there I'd been sure McKenzie was going to kick us out before we got a chance to try our hands at the case—let alone trying out any of the attractions! But Frank's mad people skillz had come through for us once again.

Everyone else seemed relieved that the tense moment was over. Well, almost everyone. For some reason, Nick was glaring daggers at Frank. Interesting. Then again, maybe he was still just nursing a grudge about the UTV.

McKenzie turned his attention to Delfina and the baby. I sidled over to Frank.

"So where do we start?" I murmured to him. "Looks like our evidence is going fast."

I nodded toward the ice. It was melting quickly in the hot summer sun.

Frank bit his lip and squinted up at the ski slopes. "It's pretty obvious where the ice came from," he said. "The question is how someone got it over here."

"Whoever did it had to have access to ice-making equipment—probably from the speed-skating track over there, or maybe the ice climbing wall or the ski slopes," I agreed, nodding toward several nearby attractions. "How hard would it be for someone to do something like this without anyone noticing?"

Frank shrugged. "Tough to say. On the one hand, there's a ton of security moving in now that all those celebs are arriving tomorrow. On the other hand, like McKenzie pointed out earlier, they're still scrambling to finish this place. Who knows how many workers have been going in and out?"

"Good point. Anyway, I guess it's not that important to know exactly how it was done. I'm more interested in why. And who had access."

"Let's see if we can talk to McKenzie about those protesters Erica mentioned," Frank suggested. "He obviously thinks they might have something to do with all this. Seems as good a place to start as any."

I nodded. "Sounds like a plan."

Unfortunately, that plan was easier said than done. McKenzie was already sending Nick off to help Delfina and the baby over to the park's first-aid center to get checked over. As soon as they were out of sight, Frank cleared his throat and stepped toward him.

"Excuse me, sir," he said. "We just need to ask you a few—"

He was interrupted by the shrill ringing of McKenzie's phone. "Hold that thought," the man told Frank before pressing the PDA to his ear. "Smith? What is it this time?"

I couldn't help noticing he sounded kind of cranky. Sort of like Smith had sounded when he was talking about McKenzie. For business partners, the two men didn't seem to like each other much.

A few seconds later McKenzie hung up with a growl. "I've got to go," he said shortly. "Keep me posted on what you find out."

"But sir—," Frank began.

This time it was no use. McKenzie strode off without a backward glance.

"Jeez," I said, watching as the man disappeared from sight behind an interactive information kiosk. "It's not going to be easy to complete this mission if the primary victim doesn't even have time to talk to us!"

Erica was the only member of the McKenzie family left. She shrugged sympathetically. "Don't take it personally. He acts like that with everyone. Even us." She grimaced. "Make that especially us."

"Bummer." I glanced at her. "Not exactly Daddy Dearest, huh?"

She shrugged again. "Not exactly. Do you guys really think you can help us? I mean, what's up with this whole ATAC thing, anyway? I never even heard of it until my father told us you two were coming."

"That's the point," I said with a grin. "It's top secret."

"Cool." Erica looked impressed. "So what other kinds of cases have you solved?"

"Listen, Erica," Frank put in before I could answer. "We were hoping to find out more about the protesters you mentioned. Can you tell us more about them?"

"I can do better than that," Erica replied. "They're out there right now. And I know a great way for you to check them out without letting them know you're doing it."

"How?" I asked.

She grinned. "It's top secret," she quipped. "Just come with me."

Okay, I was liking this girl. "Lead the way," I said.

Frank shot one last worried look at the melting ice. I guessed he was wondering if we should stick around and investigate the latest mischief a little more thoroughly. But what was to investigate? Ice was ice.

We followed Erica down the main path. Soon she cut off to one side, following one of the smaller paths. We passed a bunch of attractions we hadn't seen yet, including some kind of virtual reality thing and a drag-racing track.

Next came the huge space shuttle I'd seen from the air. It looked even cooler close up. According to the signs, it contained a zero-gravity room and a g-force simulator.

"Wow," I said, itching to get in there. "This place is amazing!"

Erica looked at me. "Yeah. My father knows how to get things done. And he was determined to make his dreams of this place come true, no matter what." Pointing ahead to the entrance to another attraction, she added, "He says he's built the longest and most exciting street luge course in the world."

Frank let out a low whistle. "Nice!" he commented.

We passed a cool-looking pipeline-style roller coaster called the Cobra and a mini-motorcycle park before Erica finally stopped at the entrance to another roller coaster, this one a more traditional design. The sign proclaimed its name to be Old Glory. It had sort of a patriotic military theme, with army uniforms and waving American flags everywhere.

"The big hill on this coaster is the highest spot in this quadrant of the park," Erica explained as she ducked under the chain stretched across the entrance. "From up there, we can see right out over the main gate."

"You mean we're going to climb up the tracks?" I asked dubiously.

She laughed. "You can hike it if you want. But I'm taking the easy way up!"

She hurried across the entryway to one of the red, white, and blue trains waiting at the edge of the platform. She hopped into the rearmost seat, then reached into her jeans pocket.

"What are you doing?" I asked as she produced a folding screwdriver.

"You'll see." She used the screwdriver to open a nearly invisible panel at the back of the car. Inside were a bunch of wires. "Come on, get in," she urged Frank and me.

We exchanged a shrug. "After you," I said.

Frank hopped into the seat ahead of Erica. I joined him, then twisted around to watch her. Her fingers flew among the complex twist of wires.

"Are you sure you know what you're doing?" I asked.

"Please keep your arms and legs inside the vehicle at all times," she recited, perfectly mimicking one of those lame announcements from every amusement park ride. Then she grinned and touched one wire to another.

With a sudden hum of power, the cars jerked into motion. We rumbled forward along the track, passing beneath the giant Stars and Stripes hanging down over the opening at the far end. Then we emerged into the open air and started climbing.

"Hang on," Erica said. "I hope you don't mind, but we have to take a few of the hills and loops before we get to the right spot."

I grinned. "We don't mind at all."

The coaster was great. Erica even made it go faster than it was supposed to around some of the hairpin turns.

"Don't worry, this thing is safety tested to twice its top speed," she shouted over the wind as we coasted up yet another hill, this one the tallest yet. "My father's just too big a wimp to push it to the limit."

I was sure McKenzie would freak out if he heard his stepdaughter say that. He didn't seem like the type of dude who'd appreciate being called a wimp.

Then we reached the top of the big hill and I forgot about that. Erica brought the car to a halt, leaving us poised up there with a great view of the entire park—and the flat, sandy landscape outside the high stone walls.

She leaned forward between us. "That's them,"

she said, pointing to a small group of people marching around in circles just outside the main gate.

There were maybe a dozen protesters. Several of them were waving signs, though I couldn't read them from that distance and angle.

"So what's their beef with this place?" I asked.

"They think it's ruining the atmosphere of the local islands, and also the environment," Frank spoke up before Erica could answer. Good old Mr. Research strikes again! "There are actually a couple of different groups involved in the protest, local and otherwise."

"That's right," Erica agreed. "It's pretty much the same bunch out there every day, though. My father thinks they'd do anything to shut him down, and frankly, I'm not so sure he's wrong."

"Can you take us out there?" asked Frank. "I think we'd better talk to them."

She paused. "I don't know," she said slowly. "They make me kind of nervous."

I glanced at her in surprise. She didn't seem like the type of girl to be scared off by a bunch of sign-waving malcontents. "Come on," I said with a grin. "It's okay—you'll be protected by the power of ATAC, remember?"

She laughed. "Well . . . okay, when you put it that way, I guess I could take you out there." A wicked glint came into her eyes. "But first we've got to get back down. So hold on!"

"Wheeeeee!" I yelled as she sent the roller coaster plunging down the huge hill. What a rush!

Soon the three of us were letting ourselves out through the security entrance beside the huge main gates, which were shut and locked. Now I could see that the protesters were mostly middle-aged people, plus two or three young hippie types. Their signs were about what you'd expect: LEAVE OUR ISLAND ALONE, the GX logo with a big X over it, stuff like that.

"Come on," Frank said. "Let's each try to talk to as many of these people as we—"

"*Aiiii!*" Erica shrieked, cutting him off. Her hand flew to her left ear. "Something just hit me in the head!"

FRANK

6

Food for Thought

"**A**re you okay?" Joe leaped to Erica's side.

I looked around. Most of the protesters were looking our way—no wonder, after Erica's piercing scream. The girl had some lungs, that was for sure.

"Did someone just throw something?" I called out.

"Not me, dude," a tall, scraggly young guy with a beard called out. "This is a peaceful protest, you dig it?"

Nearby, an elderly man with a cane shook his fist. "We're not the troublemakers here!" he cried in a thin, wavery voice. "It's that McKenzie scoundrel!"

Okay, it didn't look like anyone was going to confess. I glanced around and saw a bunch of rocks lying on the sandy ground nearby. "Which one hit you?" I asked Erica. "Did you see?"

She glanced down and shrugged. "It all happened so fast. . . ."

"Never mind," said Joe. "It's not like we can fingerprint a rock anyway."

Erica sniffled and nodded. "I'm going back in now," she said, casting a suspicious look at the protesters. "I'll leave the security door open—just make sure none of these people go in."

"We're on it," Joe assured her.

I returned my attention to the protesters as Erica disappeared back into the park. "Listen," I said to the group. "I know most of you guys are trying to be peaceful. But if one of you got carried away and threw that rock . . ."

"We told you, man. This isn't that kind of gig." This time it was a hippie chick who spoke up. She was standing by the hippie dude and holding a sign that said SEA TURTLES ARE PEOPLE TOO. "We just want to, like, express our feelings about this monstrosity, this blight on the environment." She waved a hand at the gleaming walls towering above us.

"That's right," said another woman, this one

probably forty years old, with frizzy dark hair. "Someone has to stand up for what's right."

They kept going, lecturing us on the plight of the local native species and stuff. The protesters were about evenly split. Half were locals who resented this huge change in their quiet island lifestyle. The rest were environmentalists, mostly from elsewhere, who were concerned about the effect on the ecosystem, the energy drain, the added danger from hurricanes, and more. I had some sympathy for their cause, but listening to them wasn't helping our mission much.

I exchanged a look with Joe. McKenzie thought these people were behind his problems. And it did seem possible they were behind the graffiti and that one of them had just tossed something at Erica. But how could any of them have sneaked inside and messed with the ice machines or tampered with that UTV? Was this a real lead or just a sideshow?

"So what do you think?" Joe asked as we headed back inside a few minutes later, pulling the security door shut behind us and nodding to the guard on duty. "Think any of those people could be the one we're after?"

I shrugged. "They did seem pretty worked up. But with GX's tight security . . ."

Just then my cell phone rang. It was Tyrone McKenzie. "Find anything yet?" he asked in his abrupt way.

"We're working on a few leads, sir," I replied. "Nothing concrete yet."

"All right." He sounded disappointed. I guess he'd expected us to magically solve the case in the hour and a half or so since we'd last seen him. No surprise there—"patient" wouldn't be the first word to spring to mind to describe him. Or the forty-seventh word, either.

"But it would be helpful if we could sit down and speak with you about the case," I said. "We have a few questions."

"Deal," McKenzie said right away. "Actually, I was about to invite you two to come to my family quarters for dinner tonight. Six o'clock."

It sounded more like an order than an invitation, but I wasn't complaining. Maybe we'd finally be able to talk to McKenzie for more than three seconds at a time.

"Six it is," I said. "We'll see you then."

I hung up and filled Joe in. "It's five thirty already," he pointed out. "That just gives us time to find our own quarters and wash up."

He had a point. An employee had whisked our bags away as soon as we'd disembarked from son Nick kept staring at me from his seat across from Joe. No, not just staring—glowering. He barely ate a thing.

Joe kept staring too. But I could tell he was trying to keep from laughing. Nice. A decent brother might have jumped in, maybe tried to distract McKenzie from turning things into the Frank Show. But Joe just smirked away the whole time and chatted with Delfina and Erica.

I tried a few times to change the subject to our investigation. "So we met some of the picketers a little while ago," I told McKenzie. "They seem pretty angry about this whole theme park."

He grunted. "Those losers?" he said dismissively. "I don't know what they're complaining about. They should thank me for bringing some actual business and culture to this tiny backwater of theirs."

I could give him the business part, though I wasn't too sure Galaxy X really counted as "culture." "I understand," I said. "But if they're determined to drive you out of business at any cost—"

"They don't have the guts," McKenzie broke in with a wave of his hand. "The more I think about it, the more I think all these mishaps are just bad luck. And a few sour apples from some online troublemakers, of course—but that's just free pub-

the chopper earlier. And we were looking pretty grungy after wandering around all afternoon in the hot sun—not to mention jumping out of a speeding UTV.

We walked back to the office building. The same security guard, Wallace, was on duty at the door.

"I think you guys are staying in one of the guest cottages over behind the staff quarters," he said, pointing the way. "Want to borrow one of the UTVs to get there?"

I shuddered. "No, thanks," I said, guessing he hadn't heard about our accident. "We'll walk."

The guest cottage wasn't far, and our bags were waiting for us right inside. The theme of the park extended even here, and I practically had to drag Joe away from the state-of-the-art video game console hooked up to a huge flat-screen TV. But by five of six, we were cleaned up and hurrying down a winding path toward McKenzie's house.

"I hope McKenzie turns off his cell phone long enough for us to get some info out of him," Joe said as we came within sight of the house, an angular contemporary with huge expanses of glass overlooking the back of one of the park's enormous wave pools.

"I hear you." I squinted up at the house. The windows reflected the setting sun back at me like a giant set of mirrored sunglasses. "Because so far we don't have a whole lot to go on."

"Right," Joe agreed. "And the way McKenzie's been rushing off every time we see him, I'm starting to think *he* should be a suspect!"

I knew he was kidding, but I nodded thoughtfully. "Now that you mention it, what if McKenzie's having financial trouble or something? Erica said he wanted to make his dreams come true here no matter what. And his business partner seems kind of unhappy, plus McKenzie took a call from his insurance guy earlier. . . ."

Joe's eyes widened. "You think he could be in the hole and trying to find an easy way out?"

"Who knows?" I shrugged. "Seems as decent a motive as any, if there's any truth to it."

Joe was silent for a second, mulling it over. "I don't know," he said. "If McKenzie were really behind this, why would he call in ATAC to investigate? I still think that Smith dude is a more likely suspect. He practically shoved us into that messed-up UTV."

"Yeah, he's definitely still on the list," I agreed as we headed up the shell-lined front walk. "Along with whoever's writing all those nasty blogs and stuff online."

We had to clam up about the mission then. A butler-type guy had just opened the doo[r]
house. "Frank and Joe Hardy?" he said. [Come] come in. Mr. McKenzie is expecting you."

Soon he was showing us into a swanky dining [room] with two floor-to-ceiling glass walls. The entire [fam]ily was already seated.

"Come on in, fellows," McKenzie boom[ed] from his seat at the head of the table. "Saved you [a] couple of seats here by me."

He gestured to the two seats directly to his right. Joe started toward the first one, but McKenzie half stood and grabbed my arm, pulling me that way instead.

"Why don't you sit right here, son?" he told me, yanking my arm so vigorously that I ended up accidentally stomping on Joe's foot.

"Sorry, bro," I said, reaching for the seat.

Joe smirked. "No problem, *son*."

Okay, I admit it. It was a little weird that McKenzie had taken such a shine to me. I guess it was because I'd stood up to him earlier. I had a feeling not many people did that.

He spent most of the meal grilling me abou[t] my past ATAC exploits. That was a little uncom[for]table. Partly because we're not supposed to ta[lk] about our missions—current or past—with an[y]one outside the group. Also because McKenz[ie]

licity for me." He let out a short, derisive laugh.

I traded a quick look with Joe. This was certainly a major change of tune from earlier, when McKenzie had been ready to call in the FBI. Could my theory be right? Could he possibly be behind the mischief himself and trying to throw everyone off the track?

"But listen, Frank." McKenzie leaned forward, staring at me curiously. "I want to hear more about your teen crime-fighting adventures. Who was the toughest thug you ever brought down on one of your ATAC missions?"

I sighed. "I'm really not at liberty to talk about specifics," I repeated for about the fifteenth time. "But in general, we just try to figure out who's behind any trouble and leave the actual bringing down to the authorities. . . ."

It was almost a relief when Mr. Smith barged in a few minutes later. "Tyrone," he barked. "We need to talk." He shot a glance at the rest of us, who were staring. "Business," he added succinctly.

McKenzie blew out a long, irritated sigh. "I suppose it can't wait until after dessert?" he said, his voice dripping with sarcasm.

Smith just let out sort of a low growl and spun on his heel. McKenzie dropped his cloth napkin on the table and pushed his chair back. "I'll be right back," he said distractedly, then hurried out.

"Oh, dear," Delfina murmured. "I do hope there's nothing wrong. It's not like Jack to interrupt dinner!"

"I'm sure it's nothing," Erica said, rolling her eyes. "Just Dad and his type A buddies freaking out over their balance sheets or whatever."

Nick snorted. "Right," he muttered, still glaring at me.

It seemed like a good time to focus on my food. There was a quiet moment at the table. In the silence, we could all clearly hear raised voices from the next room.

Joe and I looked at each other. Straining my ears, I tried to hear what the argument was about. But the men's words were muffled by the walls. And a moment later came the sound of stomping feet—and then a slamming door.

Space Race

"I wish we knew what McKenzie and Smith were arguing about," Frank said as the two of us hurried along the maze of shell-lined paths leading to the main part of the park.

"You and me both, dude. I can't believe he never came back to dinner." I smirked. "Not even to say good night to his favorite new adopted sonny boy."

"Enough already," Frank muttered, his cheeks going red.

I grinned. He was so easy to mess with!

Dinner had ended a few minutes earlier, and I was glad. Not that the food wasn't great—it was. And sitting next to Erica wasn't so shabby either.

The more I talked with that girl, the more I liked her. She wasn't just cute. She was supersharp, too.

Still, we weren't getting anything done sitting around eating sirloin tips and sipping iced tea. So Frank and I had excused ourselves as soon as we could. Now we planned to check out more of Galaxy X. The celebrities were due to start arriving first thing in the morning, and we wanted to make sure we had the lay of the land before then.

"Good thing it stays light so late this time of year," I said. "Come on, let's go this way—I want to check out the arcade."

"We don't have time for video games," Frank warned.

"Thanks, Aunt Trudy," I said. "Are you going to remind me to eat my peas and finish my homework, too?"

"This is serious," said Frank. "No matter what McKenzie seems to think, somebody is putting people in danger here. Somebody could have been killed by that malfunctioning UTV."

"Right," I said. "Us."

Frank wasn't finished. "That and the ice trick shows that whoever's doing this has access. And if those message board posts are any indication, things are only going to get worse tomorrow."

"Yeah, I know." I shook my head. "It's hard to believe someone would waste so much effort trying to shut this place down, isn't it?" My gaze wandered from the alien-themed pendulum ride we were passing to the blinking neon signs over the arcade just ahead. "I mean, GX is awesome!"

Frank shrugged. "To us, maybe. But you have to admit, those protesters have some legitimate gripes. Sounds like McKenzie bullied through the permits and stuff to get this place built here."

"What, are you going granola on me, bro?" I teased. "Seriously, though, are you saying you think the protesters are our main suspects?"

"I'm not sure. They have the motive, but do they have the opportunity?"

"Good point." I shot a longing glance through the big archway leading into the arcade. Most of the games were dark, but the place still looked amazing. "The ice thing almost had to be an inside job. Which leads us back to someone like Smith, or possibly McKenzie himself. But what about those anti-GX bloggers? Is there a connection there?"

"Who knows?" Frank rubbed his chin thoughtfully. "Anyone with a computer could make up a screen name and write anything they want. For all we know McKenzie himself could be that Skater Hater guy."

We continued to discuss the case as we wandered around, checking out some areas of the park we hadn't seen yet. But we hadn't reached any new conclusions by the time it got dark. The lights all stayed off—guess they were saving on the electric bill until opening night—so we had little choice but to head back to our cottage.

Inside, I made a beeline for the video game console. Meanwhile Frank pulled out his laptop and logged on.

"Anything new?" I asked as I scrolled through the impressive list of available games.

"Just the usual," said Frank. "A few new posts here and there reminding people that Preview Daze starts tomorrow, and talking about writing protest letters to the celebrities involved, or . . . Hold on!"

I looked up from the TV screen. "What?"

"Check this out."

I hurried over. The STOP GX! message board was up on the computer screen. "Is it something from that Skater Hater dude?"

"Nope. This one's an anonymous posting—no screen name." Frank pointed.

2nite's the nite this protest is really going 2 take off, the message read. *3 . . . 2 . . . 1 . . . BLAST!*

"Whoa," I said. "That sounds kind of, you know, specific."

Frank nodded grimly. "Exactly what I thought," he said. "There's been tons of ranting and raving all over the Net. It's possible this is just more of the same. But . . ."

"Maybe not," I finished for him. "The poster seems to be saying that something's going down tonight. We'd better check it out."

"Agreed." Frank logged off and stood up. "I'm thinking we should take a stroll over to that replica space shuttle."

"I hear you." The space shuttle had been my first thought too. I grabbed a flashlight from my bag. "What else could they mean by that three-two-one blastoff thing?"

"Actually, it didn't say 'blastoff,'" Frank reminded me. "It said 'blast.'"

I realized he was right. "Are you thinking what I'm thinking?"

He checked his watch. "I'm thinking it's after ten p.m.," he said. "If there's a countdown to some kind of bomb tonight, we'd better get moving."

We rushed back across the park. The beams of our flashlights lit our steps for most of the way. But as we neared the space shuttle attraction, a bright glow took over. It was lit up like a tree on Christmas morning. All the neon and bright spotlights gave plenty of light to read the message scrawled on the smooth white expanse of the shuttle's side in three-foot-high red letters:

GX IS A REAL BLAST, SO GET READY 2 FLY 2 THE MOON!

Zero Gravity

"Come on!" Joe exclaimed. "We can't let that bomb go off, or this whole place could go up!"

He gestured off to our left. Glancing that way, I gasped. He was right—only a narrow path separated the space shuttle attraction from several huge fuel tanks lined up along the edge of the drag-racing track. If they blew, the whole park could go sky-high!

I followed Joe as he raced toward the shuttle. Several steps led up to an arched entrance cut into its side. Inside, big glowing signs pointed the way to two separate attractions—the zero gravity room and the g-forces section.

"Should we split up?" I asked.

Joe nodded. "I'll go this way," he said, already rushing for the doorway leading into the g-forces area.

I sprinted the other way. Soon I was at the doorway leading into the zero gravity room.

Now, even Tyrone McKenzie couldn't build a true zero gravity facility in an amusement park. That would be impossible, at least according to what I knew about the laws of physics. What GX called the zero gravity room was actually one of those vertical wind tunnels people use to practice skydiving. Basically, a huge fan blows air straight upward through a big tube. A person can step off a platform into this airstream and the force of the blowing air holds them aloft, allowing them to "fly"—and thus feel sort of weightless.

The roar of the huge fans was audible before I reached the door. Whoever had turned on the lights must have turned on everything else at the same time. I thought about looking for the controls and turning off the fans. After all, it would be a lot easier to search the tunnel that way.

But I wasn't sure how much time we had. So I did the only thing I could do—I opened the door and stepped through it.

Trust me. Flying isn't as easy as the birds make it

look. At first I found myself sort of cutting through the wind, immediately falling several yards down toward the floor. Worse yet, a quick glance downward showed that the safety netting had been pulled away and left crumpled at the edge of the hard concrete ring around the giant fan blades!

"Whoa!" I yelped, my words instantly carried away by the whooshing wind all around me. None of our ATAC training had prepared me for this!

However, my training *had* taught me to keep my cool—and to control my body. Spreading out my arms like wings, I soon figured out how to manipulate the air currents to keep myself stable. Before long I could stay in one place or move around by tumbling or swimming through the air. It was pretty awesome!

But I wasn't there to have fun, and I didn't let myself forget it. Easing down as close as I could to the fan, I grabbed the netting and yanked it up, peering into its folds to see if anything was hidden there.

As soon as I was satisfied that there was no bomb in the net, I floated and tumbled upward through the blowing air. I examined the walls carefully all the way to the top. It didn't take long. They were padded but smooth. Nothing hidden there.

I glanced down, uneasily wondering if there was

any chance the bomb was hidden down inside the enormous fan. If it was, I figured there was no way I'd be able to find it from here. So I maneuvered over to the doorway, grabbing the threshold and pulling myself back onto the platform.

It felt weird to be out of that rushing air tube. My legs were a little wobbly as I hurried back across the lobby to see if Joe had found anything.

When I reached the door to the g-forces room, I saw that someone had turned it on as well. Looking through the viewing window, I saw that Joe was plastered against the rapidly spinning wall, the g-forces holding him in place halfway between the padded floor and ceiling. He was crawling like a spider, reaching out for something a couple of yards ahead. . . .

"The bomb!" I gasped. I'd just spotted a shoebox-size black thing with wires sticking out all over it.

How long would it take him to reach it? How long did we have? I didn't know the answer to either question. And I wasn't about to sit around pondering them either. If I could find the controls to turn off the spinning room, Joe could get to that bomb a lot faster. Racing across the viewing area to a door marked EMPLOYEES ONLY, I yanked at the doorknob.

No dice. It was locked.

Another glance toward the viewing window showed Joe still inching toward the bomb. He was only a few feet away now. But what could he do when he reached it? It would take him ages to inch his way back over to the door. Not to mention how risky it would be for him to try to get through it while the ride was moving—especially holding a live bomb!

No way. I couldn't let my brother take that kind of chance. I had to figure out a way to stop the ride's spinning.

"Aha!" I shouted as I glanced around. Right there in the viewing area was a fire alarm—complete with one of those axes encased in glass!

I leaped over and smashed through the glass with my elbow. Ignoring the sudden wail of the alarm, I grabbed the ax and raced back to the employees-only door.

It took only a couple of swings to bust through the door's cheap plywood. So much for NASA standards! I yanked the door open.

Another quick glance over my shoulder showed me that Joe had grabbed the bomb. It was tucked under one arm as he slowly made his way back across the wall.

I watched him for a moment, hoping he didn't accidentally set it off. Then I dove into the control room behind the busted-up door.

Luckily, McKenzie seemed to assume his employees would be total morons. Everything was super clearly marked, including a big red button that read EMERGENCY CUTOFF.

I punched the button. There was a squeal of machinery as the ride suddenly screeched to a stop.

"Oof!"

I winced as I heard my brother hit the floor hard. Oops. What if the sudden stop and fall jostled the bomb into going off? Bracing myself, I waited for the explosion.

Instead I heard the sound of the ride's door banging open. I rushed back out into the viewing room just in time to see my brother emerge, white-faced, with the bomb still tucked under one arm.

"Ten seconds!" he shouted, racing for the outside door.

Cowboy Up

"Ten seconds? Don't do anything stupid!" I heard Frank yell after me.

But there was no time to stop and have a discussion about our options. I'd gotten a look at the countdown clock on the side of the bomb when the g-force ride had stopped. Just in time to see the countdown click from thirteen seconds to twelve. Assuming it had taken me a couple of seconds to leap to my feet and race out the door, that gave me barely enough time to get the bomb outside—and as far away as possible from those fuel tanks—before it went *boom*.

I was vaguely aware of the shrill wail of some kind of alarm drifting out behind me as I sprinted through the hallway into the space shuttle lobby. We'd left the outside door open. I cleared the steps outside in a single leap, landing hard on the path.

I'd already worked out what to do. Veering hard to the right, I raced toward the man-made lake at the base of Mount McKenzie. It was a good fifty yards away, but I was pretty sure I could make it. . . .

"Joe!" Frank shouted from somewhere behind me.

But I didn't dare look back. Out of the corner of my eye, I could still see the counter clicking down. Four . . . three . . . two . . .

"Aaaaaaah!" I shouted, hurling the bomb away from me with all my might.

SPLASH! It landed in the water.

I turned away and flung myself to the ground. My cheekbone scraped painfully against the rough paved path. Throwing my arms up over the back of my head, I braced myself for the explosion.

Then I waited. And waited. A few more seconds passed. Waited. Nothing.

Finally I cautiously lowered my arms and sat up. Peering toward the lake, I saw its flat, smooth surface shimmering back at me, undisturbed. Had tossing the bomb in the water shorted it out or something?

I was climbing to my feet when Frank skidded to a stop beside me. "What happened?" he asked breathlessly. "It didn't go off?"

"Guess not." Somewhere nearby, I could hear shouts and running footsteps mixed in with the racket of the fire alarm. "Sounds like someone's coming to the rescue."

"Yeah. There's probably an automatic alert that went off with the fire alarm." Frank raised one hand to wave to the group of men now rushing around the corner of the nearest snack bar. "Let's just hope the security team includes someone with some bomb expertise."

As it turned out, it did. One of the security guys was an ex–bomb squadder. I showed him where I'd thrown the bomb. He made all the rest of us stand way back while he waded in and retrieved it.

Then came more waiting while he hunched over it and we all watched from a distance. Did I mention I hate waiting?

This time, though, the wait wasn't very long. After about thirty seconds, the bomb squad guy stood up and waved us in.

"Is this some kind of joke?" he asked.

I blinked. "Huh?"

He waved a hand at the soggy black box. "This

is no bomb," he said with a frown. "It's just a black metal box with some wires stuck to it. Along with a kitchen timer."

Frank and I exchanged a surprised look. "It's fake?" Frank asked.

I couldn't help feeling sheepish. Fake!

"Oops," I said with a weak laugh. "Um, well, I never claimed to be a bomb expert or anything. . . ."

The bomb guy was already bending over to pick up the dismantled fake bomb. But another dude, a tall guy with a crew cut who appeared to be in charge, was staring at us suspiciously. "Who exactly are you? And what are you doing out here after hours?"

Okay, Frank and I aren't amateurs. We gave Crew Cut our cover story. We also managed to convince him that we were so psyched at being there that we'd sneaked out to explore the park at night. And that we then just happened to see the lit-up space shuttle and stumbled onto the bomb.

I wasn't sure all of the guys totally believed it. Some of the night guards seemed a little sharper than that Wallace guy from the day shift. Crew Cut asked us a few more questions but finally dismissed us.

"Should we stay and poke around for clues?" I

murmured to Frank as we walked away. Behind us, I could hear that Crew Cut was already on the phone to McKenzie.

"I don't think so. These guys are already suspicious, and we don't want to blow our cover."

He had a point. We kept moving.

As we walked back across the darkened park, I couldn't stop thinking about what had just happened. Who would plant a fake bomb?

"Somebody's really messing with us," I commented.

Frank nodded. "We already know whoever's doing this isn't afraid to hurt people," he pointed out. "Just because this bomb was fake doesn't mean the next one will be."

When we got back to our cottage, Frank hit the Internet again. He'd barely logged on before he let out a grunt of dismay.

"An e-mail just came through," he said. "It's from Skater Hater."

"How'd he get your addy?" I exclaimed, rushing over for a look.

"Good question," said Frank grimly.

The message was short and sweet: *Just wait until next time!*

"Okay, sounds like he knows what just happened," I said. "So much for McKenzie's theory that the anti-GX bloggers are just full of hot cyber-air."

"Yeah." Frank's fingers were flying over the keyboard. "Let's see if we can trace this e-mail. . . ."

But it was no use. The e-mail address didn't lead anywhere or tell us anything about who had sent it—or from where. All we could do was forward it to ATAC HQ for more expert analysis.

"I'm sure they'll have something for us in the morning if there's anything to find." Frank stretched and yawned, glancing at the digital clock on the big-screen TV. "We might as well hit the sack. I have a feeling tomorrow could be a very long day."

"Check it out," Frank said. "Isn't that the lead singer of Mr. Nice Guyz? What's his name again?"

"Dude, who cares about some boy bander?" I glanced briefly at the singer, who was surrounded by reporters, and then returned my attention to the rest of the crowd. "There's the guy from the last Batman movie—and the star QB from this year's Super Bowl. I wonder when Cody Zane will get here?"

We'd been hanging out near Galaxy X's main gates since early that morning. That was when the media had started to pour in. I'd recognized several well-known reporters from the cable news channels, as well as a couple of famous faces from the big entertainment shows. So far it looked like McKenzie's hope for free publicity was coming true—big-time!

"Looks like a lot of the celebs are heading into the arcade," I said, watching as a hip-hop star, a couple of young actors, and the host of a popular late-night comedy show hurried through a flashing neon doorway nearby. "Should we go in and rub shoulders?"

"I don't think so." Frank's eyes darted back and forth as he tried to take in everything at once. "We can keep a better eye on things from out here. After what happened last night, I don't want to take any chances on missing something important."

I sighed, suspecting he wasn't only thinking about that fake bomb. He was still wigged out about that e-mail from Sk8rH8r. On the one hand, I saw his point. Nobody was supposed to know who we really were or why we were really there. How had this Sk8rH8r dude tracked down our e-mail?

On the other hand, it wasn't *that* weird. Frank had posted a few things on a couple of the anti-GX blogs, digging for information. For all we knew, Sk8rH8r might have phished his addy from one of the sites and sent that message to everyone.

Just then Tyrone McKenzie strode into view. He was immediately mobbed by cameras and celebrities.

That made me think of another theory. "Hey, what are the chances this is all just some big publicity stunt?" I said to Frank.

"Huh?" Frank was watching McKenzie too.

I shrugged. "Think about it. McKenzie could be Skater Hater himself. He'd have your e-mail address. And you heard what he said yesterday about free publicity. What if he's playing us? What if he's behind everything himself? He certainly has the access, right?"

SUSPECT PROFILE

Name: Tyrone McKenzie

Hometown: New York City, additional homes in other cities.

Physical description: Age 47, 5'11", 180 lbs., brown hair/eyes.

Occupation: Media mogul, theme park entrepreneur.

"If that's the case, why in the world would McKenzie call in ATAC?" Frank sounded skeptical. "It's one thing if his motive is insurance or something. Having us here gives him cover—makes it look like he's really trying to solve the problem. But if he's just after publicity, he'd be a fool to take the risk of us finding him out. And whatever other faults he might have, I think it's safe to say that Tyrone McKenzie is no fool."

He had a point. "Whatever," I said. "It was just a thought. Anyway, I'm starting to think that even if all this *is* for real, it's just some lame cyberprotest."

"But the UTV . . . ," Frank began.

"Yeah, there's that," I broke in. "But think about it. If I hadn't been driving, er, creatively, even that wouldn't have been such a big deal."

"Hmm. You may be right." He frowned at me. "At a normal rate of speed, we probably just would've ended up bumping into a tree or a trash can and getting shaken up a bit."

"Exactly. The ice thing wasn't likely to get anyone killed either."

"It might have," Frank argued. "What if Delfina had landed on the baby?"

"Thanks, Mr. Worst Case Scenario. My point is, nobody's really gotten hurt."

"Yet," Frank added succinctly. He'd already gone back to scanning the crowds.

I rolled my eyes. The preview opening was fun so far, but Frank was kind of a downer. "Why don't we split up?" I suggested. "We can cover more ground that way. You know—to watch for anything suspicious."

"Good idea," Frank agreed. "Why don't you head deeper into the park? I'll stick around here and watch who comes and goes."

"Deal." I hurried off before he could change his mind. Wandering around checking out the park definitely sounded more interesting than standing there all day.

I headed out, keeping an eye peeled for anything suspicious. But all I saw was a bunch of famous people having a blast. All the celebrities seemed to be having a great time so far. There were several people testing out the BMX bikes, and a group heading for a crazy-looking ride called the Whirligig. I even stopped and watched while a well-known gossip columnist crawled up the beginner-level climbing wall with several celebs cheering her on. From what I could tell, she'd lost some kind of bet.

A while after that I found myself in the area of the park known as the Wild Wild West. It had a cowboy-type theme, with a big shooting gallery and the Old Glory roller coaster Erica had taken us on the day before. Right in the middle was the building called the Saloon, which Frank and I had passed a couple of times yesterday. Seeing several famous faces heading in through the swinging doors, I decided it was time to check it out.

There were several attractions inside the building, but at the moment everyone was gathered around the mechanical bull in the main room. I recognized two or three actors, a famous snowboarder known only as Chill, and the guitarist for a hot new punk band called 2 Hostile. A guy with media tags was filming all of them with a digital video camera.

"What's the holdup?" the punk guy was shouting with a laugh. "Come on, I'm ready to ride the range, man!"

"I can't get it to work." One of the actors was

poking at the controls on the wall nearby. "It's busted!"

The snowboarder, Chill, hurried over. "No way, dude. This place is brand-new. You must be doing it wrong."

There was a little more argument and laughter. A couple of the others tried the controls. Still no luck.

I wandered closer, eyeing the mechanical bull. It looked like fun.

"Mind if I take a look?" I said. "Maybe I can figure out how to get it working."

One of the actors turned to look at me. McKenzie had given me and Frank name tags with our names and RADIO CONTEST WINNER printed on them. Apparently there were a few real contest winners wandering around too.

"Sure, give it a whirl." The guy stepped back and waved a hand at the controls.

I took my turn fiddling with them. But I couldn't get the thing to work either. A few of the wires seemed to be loose. It was tempting to try reconnecting them at random until something worked, but I didn't want to short the thing out completely. Or electrocute myself, for that matter.

"Sorry," I said. "Looks like this thing's really busted. I heard not everything at the park's up and running yet—maybe this is one of the stragglers."

"What?" the punk guy exclaimed with mock annoyance. "You mean they brought us in here and this place isn't even finished?"

Out of the corner of my eye, I saw McKenzie's business partner, Jack Smith, enter the Saloon. Instead of his usual somber suit, Smith was dressed in khakis and a button-down linen shirt. It didn't look natural on him. He was wearing a name tag too.

"Hello, everyone," he said. His tone was jovial, though it sounded kind of forced. "Having fun?"

"We were." Chill shrugged. "But we were in the mood for a ride and got totally denied!"

"Yeah. Way lame!" The punk guitarist raced over and vaulted onto the mechanical bull, waving one skinny arm over his head like a cowboy. I didn't bother to tell him he was sitting backward on the thing.

"It looks like some wires got messed up somehow," I offered. "A few of them are just hanging loose."

"Sounds like something Erica could take care of in her sleep," Smith said, whipping out his cell phone. "I'll give her a call."

"Erica?" I said. "You mean McKenzie's stepdaughter?"

Smith nodded. "She can fix anything."

Now that he mentioned it, I vaguely remembered

Nick making a similar comment. I couldn't help being more impressed with Erica than ever. It wasn't every hot girl who was also a Ms. Fix It!

Unfortunately, Erica didn't answer her phone. "Sorry, boys," said Smith, hanging up and then immediately dialing another number. "I'll see if I can get one of the engineers to come check it out. Shouldn't be more than half an hour."

It turns out that celebrities aren't very patient. At least these particular ones weren't. As soon as Smith left, Chill headed for the control panel again.

"Look, there's got to be a way to get this thing working," he said. "Can't be any harder than jump-starting a car, and I've done that a million times."

"I'm not sure you should do that," I spoke up as he started touching random wires together.

Okay, I know, that makes me totally sound like Frank. And I hated the thought of looking like a dweeb on camera—the media guy was still filming the whole scene. Still, I couldn't help imagining what would happen if Chill accidentally sent ten thousand volts through himself or something. That would be totally *not* chill. In more ways than one.

"Relax, dude," the snowboarder said with a laugh. "I like living on the edge."

"Hey!" one of the actors shouted. "That's it!"

Sure enough, the row of lights on the edge of the mechanical bull had just blinked on. When Chill touched the controls, the bull slowly started to revolve and buck up and down.

The punk guy had climbed down by now. "All right!" he cheered. "Who's first? Dare ya, L.A." He pointed to one of the actors with a grin.

"Me? What about you?" the actor taunted in return.

I grinned. The bull looked like fun. If none of the celebs had the guts to try it, I was ready to step up and show them how it was done!

"Hey, I got it going—I get to try it first." Chill pushed his way past the rest of us.

He vaulted easily onto the slowly turning bull. It was weird. I knew the thing was totally fake. But it seemed to react to his weight like a real animal, immediately picking up speed.

"Yee-haw!" Chill cried as the others cheered.

"Ride 'em, cowboy!" one of the actors cried. "Here, let's give you more of a challenge."

He turned the controls from level one to level two. The bull started bucking and spinning faster and harder.

"That's the stuff!" Chill yelled with a grin.

I laughed. But at the same time, I couldn't help

noticing that the mechanical bull was still picking up speed—even though the actor had dropped his hand from the controls. It spun faster and faster, bucking up and down and back and forth like crazy.

"Whoa," the guy with the video camera whispered to himself, moving a little closer for a better shot.

"Okay, okay," Chill exclaimed breathlessly. "That's enough. Turn it down."

"Wuss," the actor joked. But he complied, reaching over and spinning the dial back down to one.

There was just one problem. The bull didn't respond—except by going even faster! Soon it was spinning around like a top, still bucking. I was amazed that Chill was still holding on.

"Hey!" he shouted, sounding nervous. "Cut it out, you guys. Stop this thing before I come off!"

"I'm trying!" This time the actor pushed the dial all the way to off. But it still didn't respond.

Something was wrong here. "Hang on!" I shouted, lunging for the wires to yank them out again.

SPLAT!

I was too late. Chill had finally lost his grip. The mechanical bull had just flung him off—headfirst into the wall beside me.

FRANK

10

Spinning Wheels

I was watching some celebrities test out the snow-boarding slopes when I saw several paramedics rush past. Uh-oh. That couldn't be good.

Following them, I rounded a corner just in time to see them disappear inside the Saloon. Wallace, the pudgy security guard Joe and I had met yesterday, was just coming out. He looked pale.

"What's going on?" I asked, hurrying up to him.

"Nothing to worry about," he said. "Don't go in there."

Ignoring the advice, I pushed past him. The paramedics were bending over someone lying on the floor. I spotted Joe standing nearby.

"What's up?" I asked as I reached him.

"Another equipment malfunction," he replied grimly, watching as the paramedics loaded the victim onto a stretcher. The guy looked vaguely familiar, though I couldn't place him. "The mechanical bull went crazy and tossed Chill there into the wall," Joe added.

Oh, right. Now I recognized the guy. Snowboarder.

"Ouch." I glanced at the mechanical bull, which was still and quiet. "Think it was more sabotage?"

Before Joe could answer, the guy on the stretcher started struggling against the paramedics. "Hey, wait a sec, dudes," he said. Then he pointed to someone else. "You! You have to erase your camera. No way do I want that wipeout turning up on America's Lamest Blooper Videos or something."

"Please lie back, sir," a paramedic said politely. "You probably have a concussion, and you should really—"

"No, listen, I'm serious!" Chill sounded frantic. "Have a heart, dude. Erase that tape."

"I have permission to film freely during Preview Daze," the cameraman said with a slight smirk. "Everyone here signed a release to allow full access—including you."

"I don't care about the stinking release, dude."

Chill sounded angry. "You can't show anyone that video!"

Just then McKenzie hurried into the room. "What's going on here?" he exclaimed. "Wallace just called and said there'd been an accident. . . ."

As soon as he heard what had happened, McKenzie took the camera guy aside. Within moments, the footage was deleted and everyone was happy. Well, everyone except me and Joe.

"I would've liked to get a look at that film," I muttered as we watched the paramedics roll Chill out through the swinging saloon doors. "See if we could spot anything suspicious."

"I hear you, bro," Joe said. "But trust me, I was here. Nobody in the room had anything to do with it, I can pretty much guarantee that. That Jack Smith dude, on the other hand . . ."

"Smith?" I looked around, but there was no sign of McKenzie's business partner. "What about him? You think he had something to do with this?"

Joe grabbed me by the arm. "Come on. Let's go outside where we can talk without being overheard."

Soon we were outside across the path from the Saloon. That was when Joe told me all about what had happened in there. Including the part about Smith coming by.

"Wow," I said. "That guy always seems to be around when things go wrong."

"Exactly what I was thinking." Joe nodded. "First the UTV, now this. He has full access to the entire park at all hours, so he could've planted that fake bomb, too, and done all the graffiti and stuff."

I nodded thoughtfully, trying to figure out the angles. "Seems kind of, I don't know, juvenile for a guy like that," I mused. "But maybe that's how he's trying to throw people off. Still, I can't quite figure out how he benefits if this place tanks. Unless he and McKenzie are in on it together somehow."

"Do you really think they—oh, hello, Mr. McKenzie!" said Joe.

I spun around. McKenzie had emerged from the Saloon and was hurrying toward us. Luckily, Joe had spotted him before he got close enough to overhear what we were talking about.

"There you are," he greeted us. "What a mess, eh?" He jerked his head in the general direction of the Saloon and grimaced. "Lucky for me it was that Chilly fellow who got hurt instead of one of those prissy actors or anyone else more likely to sue me." He barked out a short, humorless laugh. "So, Frank, who do you think could have pulled off something like this?"

I felt like pointing out that we might have a better chance of answering that question if he hadn't just destroyed that video in the name of public relations. But I didn't bother.

"Well, first we should have someone look at the controls and confirm that it was intentional mischief and not just an accident," I said.

"Good point, Frank." McKenzie whipped out his handy-dandy PDA. "I'll get someone on it right away."

"Okay, but in the meantime we should probably assume it was sabotage," Joe put in. "I was there for the whole thing—there was no way that was an accident."

McKenzie glanced at him. "Hmm," he said, turning back to me. "What do you think, Frank? Do you agree with your brother's assessment?"

"Um, sure," I said. "We should certainly proceed under that assumption unless and until we find out otherwise."

"Good call." McKenzie looked pleased. "Now then, do we have any new suspects as a result of this?"

He was still staring straight at me. It was weird. Hadn't he just heard Joe say he was a witness to the whole thing? So why was he asking me all the questions?

Before I could figure out a tactful way to point

that out, McKenzie's PDA buzzed. He glanced at the screen and frowned.

"Zane's here," he said. "Come on. Why don't you two come meet him? Since a lot of the online threats seem to center around skateboarding, you'll want to keep a close eye on him. He's the center-piece of this grand opening, and I definitely don't want anything to happen to him."

Without waiting for an answer, he spun around and hurried off in the direction of the main gate. Joe and I practically had to break into a jog to keep up with him.

"I can't believe we're about to meet Cody Zane!" Joe said.

I nodded. I'd done a little research on the skate-boarder. Cody wasn't just a totally amazing athlete. He was also a marketer's wildest dream—good-looking, well-spoken, and likeable. He was up to his nose ring in major advertising and sponsorship deals. Besides that, he'd just been tapped to create his own namesake skateboarding video game. As part of the GX grand opening, he would be judging an amateur skateboarding contest. The winner got to be a character in the game.

"Is Cody Zane's partner here too?" I called to McKenzie. "What's his name—David some-thing?"

"David Sanders," Joe supplied.

"He's in Japan. Arriving in a couple of days." McKenzie sounded distracted. We'd just come within sight of the gates, and a crowd was gathered there.

Cody Zane was at the middle of it. "Wow, it's really him!" Joe exclaimed. "The real Cody Zane!"

I shot him a surprised glance. Joe and I are used to meeting celebrities by now. He doesn't usually go all fanboy over anyone. But right now he had the same look in his eye that Aunt Trudy got whenever she watched old Cary Grant movies on TV.

Soon McKenzie was introducing us. "These are two of your biggest fans," he told Cody. "Frank Hardy and his brother John."

"Joe," Joe corrected, sticking out his hand. "I'm totally stoked to meet you, Cody! Can I call you Cody?"

I had to hide a smile as I got a load of his goofy, adoring grin. Yeah. Definitely fanboy.

"Sure, man." Cody shook his hand, then mine. "It's great to meet you. Is this place tight or what?" He glanced around.

"Totally tight," Joe replied eagerly. "Want a tour? We've been here since yesterday, so we've totally got the lay of the land."

McKenzie's PDA had just gone off again. "That sounds like an excellent idea," he said, glancing at it with a slight frown. "I was hoping to show you around myself, Cody. But I'm afraid I'll have to take a rain check. You're in good hands with these two, though."

"I'm down with that," Cody said easily. "Thanks, Tyrone."

It was weird to hear him call McKenzie that. The only other people I'd heard call him "Tyrone" were Delfina and Smith.

Thinking about Smith reminded me that we still had a case to solve. I took a look at the little crowd of people still clustered nearby. It seemed to consist mostly of bodyguards and photographers.

"Look," I told Cody as soon as McKenzie was gone. "If you'd rather look around with your friends than get stuck with a couple of goofy fans like us, we understand."

"Naw, dude, it's cool." Cody grinned and slapped me on the shoulder. "I've been stuck with these losers on the plane all day. Right, guys?" He grinned over at the group.

"Yeah, get this gnarly dude out of our sight!" one of the group jeered back playfully, and several of the others laughed.

"Sweet," Joe was saying to Cody. "We should

start out at the Diamond Dragon—that's this huge vert ramp that looks totally off the hook. Then after that . . ."

I zoned out as I followed the two of them. As cool as it was to meet Cody, I couldn't really get into it like Joe was. It was bad enough knowing someone was sabotaging the park with a couple of dozen celebrities there. What would happen when the gates opened to the public in a few days and there were hundreds of innocent people in danger? True, no one had been badly injured yet, but that seemed more luck than anything else.

Or was it? *If McKenzie and Smith really are behind the mischief, it makes sense that they wouldn't want anyone to actually get killed*, I thought. *They both seem pretty ruthless, but they're not stupid. Then again, if it's not them, who knows what could happen?*

As we wandered from one half-pipe to the next throughout the park, I was itching to go over our suspect list with Joe. But he showed no sign of wanting to stop playing tour guide anytime soon. I had to settle for running over the list in my head. It was pretty sparse. Basically just Smith, McKenzie himself, or some combination of the two. Or possibly those protesters, though I still couldn't imagine how any of them could have gained the access they'd need to pull off some of these stunts.

Or it could be someone we haven't hit on yet, I thought grimly. *We really don't have much to go on other than some words on a computer screen.*

After about half an hour of trailing around after Joe and his new BFF, I thought about splitting off and going to see if the engineers had figured out anything back at the Saloon. Maybe that would give us some new clues. . . .

"Check it out," Joe was saying to Cody as they reached yet another skating fixture. "This one looks like an amazing—"

"Hey!" a shout interrupted him. "Have you seen my father?"

I turned and saw Nick racing toward us. He looked ashen faced and upset.

"Not for a while," I said. "Why? Did, um . . ." I shot a quick glance at Cody, not sure how much to say in front of him. "Did something, uh, happen?"

"I can't believe he's not answering his stupid phone!" Nick ranted instead of answering. "He goes around with that thing glued to his ear, and the one time it's really urgent he won't answer my calls or texts or—"

"Nick. Chill." Joe grabbed him by the shoulders. "Take a breath, dude." He glanced over at Cody. "Check it out—it's Cody Zane. How cool is that?"

Nick shook him off. "Whatever," he snapped. "I need to find my father. *Now*."

The look in his eyes sent a chill down my spine. "Hey, Nick, what's this about?" I asked.

"Come here." Nick grabbed me and dragged me away from Joe and Cody. His fingers dug into my arm so hard it hurt.

"What is it?" I asked when we were around the corner behind a snack bar. I shook off his iron grip. "Has there been more sabotage?"

"Worse than that." Nick swallowed hard. "Mr. Smith is dead!"

High Stakes

"**H**ey!" I blurted out when Frank suddenly reappeared and grabbed me by the arm.

"Could you excuse us for a sec?" Frank said to Cody. "Something just came up."

"No problem, dude," Cody said. "I could use a power up anyway. Catch you later!"

Did I mention Cody is awesome? Most of the celebs at the GX opening looked shorter or older or just less interesting in person. But Cody actually looked even cooler than he did in skate magazines or on TV. He was super-nice and down-to-earth, too, just like he came across in interviews.

"What's the big idea?" I complained as Frank dragged me around behind a snack bar called the

Phat Shack. Nick was standing there, leaning against the snowboard-covered wall and looking totally wiped out and weird. "I was just getting ready to show Cody the—"

"Forget about Cody for a minute," Frank interrupted, looking grim. "Smith is dead."

"What?" I immediately forgot everything else. "Smith? You mean Jack Smith, as in McKenzie's partner?"

"That's the one." Nick's voice was shaky as he answered. "Come on, I'll show you."

Frank and I followed Nick off toward Mount McKenzie. A crowd was gathered near the edge of the wave pool that lapped at the base of the Summit. That was the name of this really serious climbing wall that made up most of the sheer southeastern face of the man-made mountain.

When we got closer, we saw Smith. He was lying on the path in a puddle of water. His face was gray. I'd seen that look before. Usually on corpses.

Several paramedics were working on him. But I could tell they were giving up hope. The celebrities and media types gathered around didn't seem to realize it, though.

"Is he okay?" a well-known reality TV star called out, sounding hysterical. "Come on, bro. He's okay, right?"

The head paramedic sat back on his heels and wiped his brow. "Sorry," he said. "He's gone."

"Whoa," Frank murmured. "Looks like this mission just got a whole lot more serious."

"That's for sure," I agreed. I glanced at Nick. "So you never reached your dad?"

Nick shook his head. He appeared to be in shock. A lot of people get like that when they see their first dead body.

"I'll try him again." Frank pulled out his cell. He dialed and put it to his ear. "Oh—Mr. McKenzie?" he said a second later. "Hello, sir. I'm afraid there's some bad news. . . ."

That was weird. It sounded as if McKenzie had picked up on the first ring. So why had Nick had so much trouble reaching him?

I glanced at Nick. He was scowling at Frank. Was he wondering the same thing? Or was he angry because he realized this made him look kind of suspicious?

Filing those thoughts away to think about later, I stepped toward the onlookers. "What happened?" I asked.

"It was so weird," an actor replied in a shaky voice. "He just, like, fell!"

Frank glanced from Smith's body to the wave pool. "You mean he fell into the water?"

"Yeah," another young celebrity put in. "From the climbing wall."

"Huh?" Now I was getting confused. "Wait, you mean Mr. Smith was climbing the Summit?"

"Is that his name?" This time the speaker was the lead singer of Mr. Nice Guyz, Bret Johnston. He shrugged, making a pouty little expression that probably drove the girls wild but in my opinion made him look kind of dorky. "Yeah. Kirk here dared him to do it."

"Don't blame me, man!" The actor who'd spoken first backed away, looking nervous. "It was a joke. I didn't think he'd actually go for it! Anyway, Sanchez dared him too!" He pointed to another actor.

"I did not!" Sanchez protested.

"Did too," Bret said. "I heard you. You called him a creaky old fogey."

They all started to argue after that. But Frank and I were getting the gist of what had really happened. It sounded as if some of the young celebrities had taunted the "old fogey" into giving the climbing wall a whirl. He'd finally given in, probably in the interest of public relations. Smith wasn't exactly the freewheeling X-Gamer type or anything, but he'd appeared to be pretty fit for his age. In other words, perfectly capable of climbing that wall even if he didn't enjoy it much. And it sounded like he'd done fine until he was about halfway up.

"Then he just, like, lost his grip or something," Kirk explained with a shudder.

"Yeah," Bret agreed. "It was like he just fell straight backward. Totally weird."

"Maybe he had a heart attack!" said Sanchez hopefully. "That would mean it wasn't our fault."

Frank rubbed his chin thoughtfully. "It's not your fault either way," he said. "Smith was a grown man. He chose to make that climb. He could've refused if he didn't think he could handle it." He squinted up at the climbing wall. "But listen, the wave pool is supposed to be a safety feature. A fall from that height into the water shouldn't have been enough to kill him."

An actor whose name I didn't know shook his head. "That's what we thought."

"Yeah. We were all laughing and cheering and stuff," Sanchez said with a guilty grimace. "That's why it took us a minute to notice he wasn't coming up."

Bret shrugged. "Guess he couldn't swim." He pointed to another member of the group, a well-known Olympic swimmer. "Gold Medal here dove in and pulled him out, but by then it was, you know . . ." He nodded toward the body, which the paramedics had just covered with a sheet. "Too late."

Just then McKenzie arrived with several security guards in tow. He spoke quietly with the paramedics, then turned to the rest of us.

"I'm very sorry about this," he said. "I regret that you had to witness this tragic accident, and I truly hope it won't mar your enjoyment of Galaxy X."

Was it my imagination? Or had his eyes lingered accusingly on Frank and me as he looked around?

McKenzie went on to invite everyone over to the arcade for complimentary pizza and the chance to win a jet ski in a video game contest. That seemed to cheer up the celebrities a little, though a few of them still looked upset as they hurried past Smith's covered body. Soon the only ones left on the scene were McKenzie, Nick, the paramedics, and the dead guy. And Frank and me, of course.

"Did you two witness this?" McKenzie snapped at us.

"I did," Nick put in. "And I think—"

"Hush, son. I'm talking to Frank and his brother now," McKenzie cut him off. Then he stabbed a finger toward Smith. "Was this more sabotage?" he asked us.

"We're not sure, sir," Frank said. "It does seem

suspicious that Mr. Smith wasn't able to survive that kind of fall with the pool as a safety feature."

McKenzie shrugged. "Nothing suspicious about that. Smith couldn't swim a stroke. Practically fainted every time he had to cross water to get to this island." He gave that humorless laugh of his.

"Well, then I suppose it might just be an unfortunate accident," Frank said. "We'll investigate and let you know what we find."

"Good." McKenzie seemed satisfied with that. "Glad to know you're on the job, Frank." His gaze wandered briefly toward me. "Er, and you too," he added. "In any case, I'd better get over to the arcade and do some damage control." He hurried off without another glance at us—or Smith's body.

"What a nice, sympathetic guy," I said sarcastically as soon as he was out of earshot. Then I realized Nick was still standing there. "Oops," I added. "Uh, sorry, bro. I just meant—"

Nick didn't seem to be listening. "Listen," he said urgently. "Mr. Smith didn't just, like, lose his grip or something. This wasn't just an accident. I saw the whole thing—that handhold came loose!"

Bad Blood

"Are you sure?" I asked Nick.

"Pretty sure." Nick looked momentarily uncertain. "I mean, I heard him yell, and then he started to fall, and something popped out of the wall and fell right beside him. It was hard to see because the sun was in my eyes, but . . ."

"Thanks, Nick," said Joe. "We'll check it out."

"Whatever." Nick watched as the paramedics loaded Smith's body onto a gurney. "You might want to mention it to my father, anyway. He's way more likely to listen if it comes from anyone except me." He scowled and stalked off.

Wow. The guy really had some issues with his father. Then again, based on the way McKenzie treated him, maybe he had a right to.

Joe and I couldn't exactly go wading into the wave pool to search for that handhold while the paramedics were still there. Not without blowing our cover, anyway. In fact, a couple of the security guards were already giving us suspicious looks.

"Come on," I said. "Maybe we should make like radio contest winners for a while. We can come back once these guys clear out."

Joe caught on right away. "Let's go on that," he suggested, pointing. "Looks like it'll give us a chance to talk in private. Plus it looks really cool."

He was pointing to a ride sticking up over the top of the demolition derby attraction nearby. It was called the Mineshaft, and it was one of those free-fall rides. The difference was that this one started high above the ground but kept dropping you deep under the ground. Then it spun you around upside down for a while. Or something. I hadn't paid that much attention when we'd passed it earlier.

"Okay," I said. It seemed as good a way as any to get some private space to discuss the mission.

A few minutes later we were strapped into our own private capsule. It was shaped like an actual old-fashioned mine cart. Compared to all the high-tech steel and polymers throughout GX, its wooden seat and sides felt a little rickety. I hoped that was just part of the effect. There were actually four seats in each cart, but luckily, we had our cart to ourselves.

"I guess this crosses Smith off our suspect list," I said as the ride creaked into motion, lifting us slowly upward.

"Yeah. Unless this really was an accident," Joe pointed out with a wry smile. "If nothing else happens, we'll know it was him."

"Doubtful." I shook my head. "It also doesn't seem too likely that McKenzie was behind this either."

"Huh? How do you figure? Those two weren't exactly getting along like best buds from what I could tell. What if Smith was, like, threatening to expose some financial shenanigans or something and McKenzie decided to bump him off?"

"Doesn't make sense." By now our cart had climbed high enough to give us a view of Mount McKenzie and the climbing wall. "How could he possibly know Smith would be the one to hit that bad handhold? You heard those guys—they dared him into it. If they hadn't, it probably would've been one of them who fell."

"True," Joe agreed. "So maybe McKenzie wasn't after Smith at all. Anyone else would've fallen, but also probably would've been able to swim. So then we'd have yet another close call. I don't see how this lets McKenzie off the hook at all." He narrowed his eyes. "Wait. Unless you just don't want to think he's the culprit because he's your number one fan?"

"Don't be an idiot." I frowned at him. "I just don't think he has a strong enough motive. He's getting plenty of free publicity already. Why would he take that kind of risk for a little more?"

"I don't know. Element of danger?" Joe shrugged. "I mean, that's what Skater Hater and the rest are complaining about, right? That GX basically defangs their beloved extreme sports. The fun without the risk. Skate culture you buy at the mall. That kind of thing."

Despite his words, I could tell he wasn't sold on the McKenzie thing anymore. He had a strange look in his eye. I was pretty sure it was thoughtfulness. Yeah. For Joe, that qualifies as a strange look.

"What?" I asked as the ride continued to rumble upward.

"I was thinking about something earlier," he said. "What about Nick?"

"What about him? You think he could have something to do with this?"

"Maybe. It's way obvious that he and his dad

aren't that close." Joe glanced at me. "What if this is his, you know, cry for attention?"

"Interesting theory." We were almost at the top of the ride by now. That gave us a panoramic view of at least half the park, including the main gates. As I glanced that way, something caught my eye. "Hey, check it out," I said, pointing. "Is that smoke coming from outside?"

"Where?" Joe asked. "I don't—AIIIEEEEEEE-EEEEE!"

At that moment the floor dropped out from under us. Or at least that's how it felt. The ride plunged us down, down, down, so fast I couldn't breathe for a second.

"Ahhhhh!" I yelled as we crashed through a ground-level trapdoor into total darkness and fell some more—and then shot suddenly sideways along a wildly twisty shaft with flashing lights and echoing screams bouncing off the walls. I had to admit, it was awesome!

Still, by the time we emerged from the ride, we were all business again. "Are you sure you saw smoke outside?" asked Joe.

"Yeah," I said. "Not a lot, but it was definitely there."

Just then we heard someone calling our names. Nick. He was stripped down to a pair of shorts and some flip-flops, and his hair was wet.

"I found it!" he called breathlessly, hurrying up to us. "See?"

He held something up—a blobby piece of plastic about the size of a donut. "What is it?" Joe asked, sounding distracted.

"The climbing handhold!" Nick said impatiently. "I went in and found it. I told you I saw it fall!"

My heart sank. This meant one of two things. Either Nick was telling the truth, and he really had found a key piece of evidence, or he'd made up that story for reasons of his own and was now trying to fake said evidence. The trouble was, we really had no way of knowing which. I wished we'd stuck around until the paramedics were gone so we could have searched for that handhold ourselves. But it was too late now.

"That's great," I said to Nick. "Why don't you go show your dad? Um, we need to check out another lead right now."

"Yeah. See you," Joe added. Then we hurried off.

I sneaked a peek back over my shoulder. Nick didn't look happy. "Uh-oh," I murmured to Joe. "He probably thinks we're blowing him off just like his dad always does."

"Well, we kind of are," Joe said. "But forget him. Let's get out to the main gate."

When we arrived, we soon realized what was causing the smoke I'd seen. One of the protesters was burning a GX poster. Namely, the old man with the cane we'd seen before. The poster was throwing up a decent amount of black smoke as it sizzled on the pavement. A local cop was standing by, keeping an eye on things but not interfering.

There weren't as many protesters as there had been the day before. The hippie couple was gone, along with several others. Most of those who were left were sitting around on the curb drinking coffee and chatting with one another. The only one who still seemed worked up was the old guy burning the poster.

"Come on, people!" he shouted hoarsely as he lit up another poster. "Are we going to let them take over our home and destroy our lifestyle?"

The frizzy-haired fortyish female protester sighed. "Don't work yourself up so much, Frederick," she said kindly. "It isn't good for your health. This protest is going to be a marathon, not a sprint."

Another woman nodded. "We just need to stay strong and convince Mr. McKenzie to compromise on some of his plans, maybe get him to donate more to the groups trying to keep the remaining natural areas of these islands pristine."

"No!" the old man cried. "That's not good enough. I'm going to shut this blight down if it's the last thing I do!" He shook his fist, then coughed. Patting his shirt pocket, he scowled. "Where's my durn heart medicine?" he muttered, searching his pants pockets. "Musta left it in the car. . . ."

He hobbled off, leaning heavily on his cane, still cursing McKenzie and Galaxy X under his breath. "Wow," Joe said as he watched him go. Then he glanced at the other protesters. "Who is that guy?"

"Oh, that's just Frederick," Frizzy Hair said with another sigh. "W. Frederick Jackson, that is. He's lived over on the next island from here his whole life. His family's been here for generations." She waved a hand in the direction of the shoreline beyond GX's parking lot. "I suppose you could call him our local crusty old bachelor."

"He seems pretty intense," I said. "I guess he really wants to shut this place down, huh?"

The woman squinted up at the walls of the theme park. "He sees this place as a threat to the only way of life he's ever known. I suppose we all do, really. But most of us are sort of resigned to it by now."

The second woman chuckled. "Yeah. Including most of Freddie's relatives," she put in. "They all felt a whole lot better once they realized the extra tourism stood to make 'em a bundle."

Interesting. Joe and I asked them a few more questions, then huddled near the entrance. "Well?" said Joe. "Think that Jackson dude could be our guy?"

"He does seem to have the perfect motive," I said. "But if he's behind the mischief, he has to have an accomplice. There's no way he could've pulled off most of it on his own."

Joe laughed. "Yeah. Even if he could figure out a way past security, I can't picture him climbing up to loosen that handhold. Or even climbing the steps up into the space shuttle to plant that fake bomb!"

"Maybe we should stick around and talk to him. And have the guys back at HQ look into him a little too," I said. "Just in case."

Suspicious behavior: Picketing outside GX; claims to be willing to do anything to shut the place down.

Suspected of: Sabotaging the park (with help from unknown accomplice/s) in order to shut it down.

Possible motives: Desire to return island to its former state; revenge for GX changing the flavor of the islands.

But before Jackson returned from his car, my cell phone rang. It was Tyrone.

"Frank. I want an update on the case," he said abruptly. "Meet me at the Summit."

"Okay, do you want—," I began. But the little click on the line told me he'd already hung up. "McKenzie wants me to come give him an update," I told Joe. "He didn't say anything about you, so I guess you're off the hook."

"Surprise, surprise." Joe smirked.

I rolled my eyes. His jokes were getting old. "Listen, why don't you find an Internet connection and e-mail ATAC about this Jackson guy?" I suggested.

"If they dig up any dirt on him, we can come interview him later."

"Will do. Have fun!"

When I reached the base of the Summit, I found McKenzie suiting up in the equipment shack. "Er, are you planning to, you know, climb the wall?" I asked in surprise.

"*We're* going to climb it." McKenzie tugged on one of his climbing shoes. "My son showed me that loose handhold. I had the guys go over it, but I want to test the wall myself and make sure it's safe. You can swim, can't you, my boy?" He clapped me on the shoulder. "Now suit up and let's go!"

What could I say? I suited up.

The meeting was tough. So was the Summit. I'd already seen that it was modeled after a deepwater soloing wall, with no ropes or nets—just a deep lagoon at the far end of the wave pool to catch anyone who fell. The handholds were molded to resemble real rock as much as possible, and the surface was rough and uneven. Within ten minutes I was sweating and banged up, with a big scrape on one knee and another on my arm.

Meanwhile McKenzie seemed to be having a ball. He was wearing long pants and sleeves, so he escaped most of the scrapes.

While we climbed, I filled him in on our latest

chat with the protesters. I also told him about W. Frederick Jackson.

"That old loony tunes?" McKenzie responded with a derisive snort. "He's just a sore loser, not any kind of threat."

"Perhaps." I winced as my hand slipped and my knee banged into the wall—again. Luckily, I caught myself before I totally lost my grip. "But we're checking him out just in case."

"Fine." McKenzie sounded impatient as he hauled himself up another few feet. "What else have you got?"

I clambered up until I was even with him again. Then I told him about the mysterious e-mail and our adventures at the space shuttle. He knew about the fake bomb, of course. But he seemed interested in the e-mail.

"Think it's from the same jerks who've been badmouthing GX all over the Internet?" he asked.

"Could be. Our HQ computer geeks are doing their best to track down some answers."

Naturally, I didn't tell him he was on our suspect list. I also left off Joe's suspicions about Nick. Until we had more to go on, I didn't want to say anything to make their relationship even worse than it already was. And of course, I skipped our earlier suspicion of Smith. There didn't seem to be much point mentioning it now.

Finally we reached the top of the wall. "Victory!" McKenzie crowed as he hoisted himself onto the platform.

"Yeah," I panted, clambering up after him. I couldn't help being impressed by how fit McKenzie was. I guess he managed to work in some time at the gym between all his business meetings.

He tossed his helmet to one of the employees working the platform. Then he strode to the edge and surveyed the park. The visiting celebrities and their hangers-on were scurrying around like insects. Rich, famous insects.

"This is great," McKenzie declared, rubbing his hands together. "We should be all over the entertainment shows tonight. Our grand opening is going to be massive! The fireworks company guarantees that the show is going to be the biggest blast anyone in this part of the world has ever seen."

"Sounds great, sir," I said. But I couldn't stop my eyes from straying downward—toward the pool where Smith had died. Had it been nothing more than a tragic accident? Or was whoever was sabotaging the park getting more and more desperate?

Because if that's the case, I thought grimly, *this place might end up seeing more fireworks than anyone is expecting*.

A Need for Speed

I tapped my fingers on the computer keyboard. I'd just sent an e-mail to ATAC HQ about W. Frederick Jackson. Now I was doing a little extra research at one of the park's Internet kiosks.

I know, I know. I usually leave that sort of thing to Frank. But I was still kind of stuck on my earlier thoughts about Nick. I just wanted to find out a little more about him.

As it turned out, McKenzie's family was incredibly easy to Google. There were all kinds of articles about them out there. I discovered that McKenzie and Nick's mom had split in a bitter divorce when Nick was a kid. She was currently married to another successful business tycoon and living in Florida.

Erica's mother hadn't been so lucky. McKenzie was actually her second marriage; her first husband was a Hollywood stuntman who'd died while shooting a video. Actually, that was how McKenzie met her—it was one of his artists' videos. The two had married a year later, when Erica was about ten, and divorced when she was fifteen. Erica's mother had died of cancer less than two years later, which was when Erica had gone to live with her stepfather.

Then there was Delfina. She and McKenzie had been married for a little over a year. There were tons of pictures of their splashy New York society wedding on the Web. I even found out how much baby Tyrone Jr. had weighed when he was born. Yeah, I was sure *that* info was going to come in handy.

None of my research did much for my suspicions one way or another. But I shot off another message to ATAC. My Google skills were okay. But I figured it wouldn't hurt to have the real experts check into Nick a little more.

SUSPECT PROFILE

Name: Nicholas Marsh McKenzie

Hometown: New York City

Physical description: 5'9", 160 lbs., reddish-brown hair, hazel eyes.

Occupation: Student, slacker, part-time club kid

Suspicious behavior: Makes it obvious that there's no love lost between him and Daddy. Only person to witness alleged handhold malfunction on climbing wall. Sabotaged UTV belonged to him.

Suspected of: Sabotaging GX.

Possible motive: A desperate cry for his father's attention.

I was about to sign off when my e-mail alert dinged. Clicking over to my in-box, I saw a new message. My eyes widened as I took in the return addy: Sk8rH8r.

The message itself was short and not so sweet: *Sk8r culture not 4 sale! B-ware or B sorry!*

"Interesting," I murmured.

I forwarded the message to ATAC. There wasn't much else I could do about it right then, so I signed off and headed back outside. Now what? I figured

Frank would call when he was out of his meeting. In the meantime, I decided to scout around for Cody Zane. I was still bummed that our tour had been cut short earlier—I was itching to do some skating with him. How cool would that be?

I checked all the skateboarding fixtures, but there was no sign of him. Finally I spotted one of his bodyguards, a beefy dude with a purple and black striped Mohawk. He told me Cody had just headed over to try out bungee jumping.

"He decided to go old school," Mohawk said with a laugh. "You should be able to catch him there."

"Thanks." I'd noticed the bungee-jumping spot earlier. It was a platform sticking out from the highest hill of one of the roller coasters.

When I got there, I found Cody already up on the platform with a couple of other celebs. A photographer or two were up there too.

"Hey," I greeted Cody. "Remember me?"

"Sure, bro." He clapped me on the back. "You got here just in time. I'm about to inaugurate this sucker!"

I glanced over at the employee working the attraction. He appeared to be trying to figure out the bungee cord's harness system. "You mean nobody's tried it yet?"

"That's what he said." Cody jerked a thumb at the employee. "I don't know why not. I can't wait to fly, man!"

"I call second go," one of the other celebs spoke up. "Can you believe they've got this here? It's totally retro!"

I grinned, but I was a little distracted. Mainly because I couldn't help recalling how taking the first spin on a GX attraction had played out for poor Mr. Smith. Glancing down, I saw that jumpers ended up dangling right over the seating area for one of the snack bars. No water landing there. I guess McKenzie and his designers counted on the cord never breaking. I could only hope they were right.

For one crazy second I almost begged Cody not to do it. But I held my tongue. If I said anything like that, it would blow my cover. Not to mention make me look like a total dork if nothing happened. Instead I sidled over to check out that cord. It looked okay—no obvious cuts or thin spots that I could see. The harness appeared to be fully functional too.

Still, I didn't relax until Cody made his jump—and ended up dangling safely at the end of the cord, whooping and hollering happily. Whew!

After that, the others started clamoring for their

turn. "You gonna give it a go, man?" Cody asked me once they hauled him back up to the platform.

"Maybe later," I said. "Actually, I'd rather go try out some of those sweet skating spots. What do you say?"

I expected Cody to be psyched for some skateboarding. But he just shrugged. "I'll be doing plenty of skating once that contest gig starts," he said. "Until then, I'd rather try out some of the other stuff here. You game?"

"Sure." I admit it, I was a little disappointed that we weren't going to skate. But I figured just hanging with Cody was pretty cool all by itself. "Where do you want to start?"

"How about ice climbing?" he said.

After what had happened to Smith, climbing wasn't exactly at the top of my to-do list. But I wasn't about to say that to Cody.

"Sounds fun," I said instead. "Let's hit it."

I was right. The ice climbing *was* fun. After that we tried out the street luge and the monster trucks. Both totally amazing.

Finally we headed over to the motocross circuit. By then I'd practically forgotten I was on a mission. And why not? Everything at GX was running smoothly. Sure, there was that weird new e-mail from Sk8rH8r. But did it really mean anything? Or was it just some Internet cowboy tossing out idle threats from his mom's basement?

It seemed as possible a theory as any. After all, Smith's fall could have been an accident. The busted UTV and the mechanical bull, too. Even the ice thing. That W. Frederick Jackson might be feeble, but even he probably could've managed to wield a can of spray paint. If he'd done the graffiti and maybe tossed that rock at Erica, that just about covered everything.

Well, not *everything*. There was still the fake bomb at the space shuttle. It was hard to imagine the old man pulling that one off. And it was weird how Frank and I had gotten that e-mail afterward. But maybe Jackson had managed to arrange it somehow, even if he hadn't done it himself. Or maybe that one had been Nick tossing in a little anti-Daddy tantrum.

I'm starting to wonder if there's really a serious mission here at all, or if ATAC sent us for nothing, I thought as I revved the engine of my bike and headed out onto the course. *Not that I'm complaining . . .*

"Hey, wait up!" I shouted as Cody zoomed off ahead of me.

He probably couldn't hear me, what with the helmets and the roaring engines. But at that moment he glanced back and shot me a thumbs-up. Then he pointed ahead. The course split and went off a few different ways. The route Cody was pointing to had a bunch of pretty challenging-looking jumps.

I grinned, gunning it after him. The first jump was a biggie. But I wasn't too worried—Frank and I ride our motorcycles everywhere. I'd done a little off-roading with mine, and I was sure I could handle anything GX threw at me.

My bike responded quickly as I hit the gas. I was just a few yards behind Cody as he reached the first jump. I was already leaning forward over the handlebars, preparing myself.

But something made me look up just as Cody crested the jump and grabbed some serious air. I gasped as I saw the front wheel fly completely off his bike!

Losing Grip

I called Joe as soon as I escaped from my meeting with McKenzie. He didn't answer. Probably turned off the ringer and forgot to turn it back on—pretty typical when he's distracted. And my brother was definitely finding GX distracting.

So I decided to track him down the old-fashioned way. It didn't take long. A bunch of people had seen him palling around with Cody Zane. No surprise there, either.

I caught up to them at the motocross course. As I stepped into the equipment shed, I was just in time to see the two of them take off onto the course.

"Want to hop on a bike and go after them?" one of the guys working the shed asked.

It was tempting. The course looked like fun. But we were supposed to be working, not playing. There was no time to lose if we wanted to close out this mission before GX opened to the public the next day.

"No, thanks," I told the guy.

I stepped outside. Joe and Cody were speeding toward a line of jumps about a hundred yards away.

Cody was in the lead. As his bike hit the arc of the first jump, my ATAC instincts kicked in. I started running as soon as I saw the wheel part ways with the rest of his bike.

After that it all seemed to happen in slow motion. I was already picturing Cody's bike crashing down and Joe landing on top of it. But Joe managed to skid to a stop at the crest of the hill.

"Nice riding, bro," I murmured, my gaze shifting back to Cody as I kept running.

Cody seemed to realize something was wrong while he was still in midair. Probably his skater instincts, combined with the weight of the wheel coming off. He pushed himself off the handlebars as the bike fell back to earth. Hitting the dirt hard on one shoulder, he tucked and rolled. He was back on his feet almost before the bike crashed down nearby.

"Are you okay?" I shouted as I ran up to him.

Joe was already there. "Don't move," he said. "Is anything broken?"

Cody ignored his advice. He was already brushing the dirt off his clothes.

"Whoa," he said breathlessly, his face pale. "Did you see that? What happened?"

"Good question." I traded a glance with Joe. It was pure luck that Cody had escaped a bad wreck. A less skilled athlete might have been seriously injured—or worse.

Meanwhile the employees and other guests who had witnessed the accident were rushing over. "Are you hurt?" shouted one of them. The voice sounded familiar. I realized it was that pudgy security guard we'd met before, Wallace.

"I think he's okay," I responded as the employees from the equipment shed swarmed around the crumpled bike.

A couple of Cody's bodyguards hustled him off to the medical center despite his protests. I couldn't blame them. Someone shouted to call Mr. McKenzie, while someone else got on the loudspeaker and ordered the other riders on the course back in. In all the confusion, Joe and I had no trouble slipping away.

"Wow, that was close!" Joe exclaimed as we

paused just outside. "Should we check for clues in the equipment shed? Maybe other bikes were tampered with."

"Nah, the employees will be on top of that," I said. "I've got a better idea. Let's go see if Mr. W. Whatever Jackson is still outside. It might be time for a serious talk with him."

We headed for the main gate. "Do you really think that old dude did this?" asked Joe, sounding doubtful.

"I don't know. I'm still not convinced he has the access. But we should figure it out for sure before we tackle the trickier suspects."

"You mean McKenzie and Son?"

"Bingo."

But when we got outside, there was no sign of any of the protesters. "Cops showed up a couple of hours ago and hauled them all off to the station," the security guard on duty reported. "Guess Mr. McKenzie talked them into taking things seriously after, you know . . ." He glanced around and added somberly, "Mr. Smith."

"So much for that," I muttered as we walked back inside.

"Still doesn't mean Jackson couldn't have done it," Joe pointed out. "Who knows how long ago that bike was messed with? There aren't many people here using the equipment yet. It's possible someone loosened that wheel hours ago—even days ago."

"True," I agreed. "But how likely is it that Jackson could've hobbled in here on his cane and done it?"

"I hear you," Joe said. "But like we were saying earlier, he could have an accomplice. Maybe one of those other protesters?"

I still wasn't totally convinced. Somehow I just couldn't imagine the polite housewives and earnest hippies we'd seen earlier pulling something like this.

"Anyway, looks like we'll have to wait on questioning any of the protesters," I said. "So what now? Want to follow up on the Nick theory?"

"For sure." Joe nodded. "Speaking of which, I found out some juicy info earlier. . . ."

He filled me in on some online research he'd done. I already knew most of the info from my own research on the way down. But I listened carefully in case I'd missed anything.

Then we set off in search of Nick. A lot of celebrities were hanging out in the main arcade, but there was no sign of McKenzie's son among them.

"A bunch of guys were talking about hitting the

mogul course," Joe said. "You know—the reality TV dudes, that Bret Johnston guy from Mr. Nice Guyz, some others. Maybe Nick's with them."

I shot him an amused look. "Getting awfully cozy with the celebs, huh?"

Joe rolled his eyes. "Come on. Let's head over to Mount McKenzie."

We approached from the "warm" side of the mountain—the half with the climbing walls. When we got there, we started around toward the skiing and snowboarding stuff on the "cold" side. As we passed an unmarked door leading directly into the fake mountain, it opened and Erica came out.

"Oh!" she said when she saw us. "Hey, guys. How's the investigation going?"

"So-so." Joe peered past her curiously. "Where's that door go? Is there stuff to do inside the mountain?"

"Nothing fun. It's just a service door," she said. "Leads back to the security station and some other behind-the-scenes stuff." She made a face. "I was hiding out from that Bret guy from Mr. Nice Guyz. He keeps hitting on me."

"Really?" Joe grinned. "Hey, I bet there are a lot of twelve-year-old girls who'd love to be in your shoes."

"Maybe. But I'm just not into it." Erica sidled

closer to me. "Want to pretend to be my boyfriend for a while?" she asked with a grin. "Maybe that'll give him the hint."

I laughed uncertainly, not sure if she was joking or not. "Um, sure. But listen, have you seen your brother? We need to talk to him about something."

"You mean Nick?" She shrugged. "Haven't seen him. Why? Is this about that loose handhold or whatever? Because he already handed it over to our father."

"Yeah, he mentioned that," Joe said. "We just need to talk to him."

Her eyes widened. "Hang on," she said. "Is Nick, like, a suspect or something? Is that it?"

Joe and I traded a glance. Oops. "Well . . . ," I began, searching my mind for a good response.

"Got it," she said. "But listen, don't waste your time. I mean, I get why you'd think of him, the way he and our father are always sniping at each other. Not to mention how he always wants to be the center of attention." She paused. "Actually, now that I think about it, I totally wouldn't put it past him to *want* to mess up Dad's plans. The thing is, there's no way he could pull it off."

"What do you mean?" asked Joe. "He has full access to the park, and—"

She held up a hand to stop him. "Yeah, that's not what I mean. See, Nick's hopeless when it comes to anything mechanical or technical. He can barely work his iPod." She shrugged. "If he tried to mess with the wiring on that mechanical bull or the steering on the dune buggy, he'd probably electrocute himself."

I remembered how everyone kept saying how good Erica was with the tech stuff. Was she just disdainful of her stepbrother because of her own superior skills? Or was she right about Nick's abilities—or, rather, *in*abilities?

"Okay, thanks," I said. "Good to know."

"You're welcome." She squeezed my arm and grinned. "Anything for you, Mr. Boyfriend."

Joe laughed. I wasn't sure what to say, so I just cleared my throat. "Er, come on, Joe. Let's go see if they finished checking over those motocross bikes yet."

We finally tracked down Nick a few hours later. Unfortunately, we didn't get anything useful out of him. All he wanted to talk about was how his dad had almost killed Cody Zane. The weird thing was, he didn't seem too clear on exactly what had happened. Either he was a better actor than I would've thought, or he hadn't had anything to do with the accident.

Joe and I talked it over when we got back to our cottage that night. "Think Erica was protecting him by talking about how clueless he is?" Joe said.

"Maybe, but I doubt it. They don't seem that close."

"So is Nick still on the list?"

"Sure, for now. Along with his father. And Jackson." I sighed, feeling frustrated. The Nick lead hadn't panned out. The protesters still weren't back. And we were running out of time. "But I feel like we're missing something, you know? Like, some key clue somewhere that'll point us to a whole new culprit."

"You sure about that?" Joe flopped down on the couch and smirked at me. "I think you're just protecting your new rich daddy, Tyrone McKenzie."

"Very funny." I glanced at the darkening windows. "The public grand opening begins tomorrow. Whoever's doing this only has one more night to make mischief. Feel like trying to catch him in the act?"

"Sure." Joe sat up and reached for one of the flashlights lying on the coffee table. "Let's go."

Soon we were skulking around GX. It was pitch-dark, thanks to the clouds covering the moon.

"This place is kind of spooky at night," Joe murmured as we approached Mount McKenzie. "Wonder what it'd be like to try snowboarding in the dark?"

"Don't even think about it," I warned in a low voice.

"Shh!" Joe hissed suddenly, cocking his head to one side. "Did you hear that?"

"What?" I held my breath. A second later I heard it: a sort of soft clunk.

Joe was already creeping toward a fence nearby. "I think it's coming from the BMX course," he whispered.

The entrance to the course was pretty far away. So we scaled the fence. We were as quiet as possible. But not quiet enough. We reached the top just in time to see a figure dressed in dark clothes and a ski mask glance up. Then he took off running in the opposite direction.

"Stop!" Joe shouted, leaping down from the top of the fence.

I hit the ground running, just a step or two behind him. I caught the dark figure in the beam of my flashlight as I ran. It looked like a fairly large guy. That was all I could tell from the back.

Just then I felt my feet start to skid out from under me. "Whoa!" I cried. "Careful, bro."

"It's some kind of grease." Joe aimed his flashlight at a large can lying on the ground where the figure had been crouching. "He was sabotaging the course so the bikes would all skid out!"

I caught the figure again with my flashlight. He was just clambering over the fence on the far side. "Come on, we've got to catch him."

By the time Joe and I vaulted over the fence, the dark figure was sprinting for Mount McKenzie. He dashed across the bridge leading to the base of the Summit.

"What's he doing?" Joe cried. "We've got him—there's nowhere to go from there!"

"Yes there is," I said grimly, my flashlight illuminating the guy as he started to climb. "Up. He's probably thinking he can scoot across at the top and escape by sliding down one of the ski tracks on the other side." I groaned, knowing what I had to do. "Why don't you run around and see if you can catch him? I've been up the Summit before—I'll follow him here."

Joe nodded. "I'm on it."

He disappeared into the darkness. I ran across the bridge and skidded to a stop at the bottom of the wall, peering up. The guy was barely visible in the darkness, scrambling from one handhold to another. There was no time to stop for a helmet or other safety equipment. Tucking my flashlight in my back pocket, I reached for the lowest handholds and started to climb.

If it had been tough climbing the wall earlier, it was ten times tougher in the dark. But I kept going, relying partly on my memory of the earlier climb. Soon I could tell I was gaining on my quarry. I could hear him just a few yards above me, grunting and panting. Was he getting tired already?

The only light came from some safety lights down by the wave pool. That was enough for me to see the guy stop and sort of turn to one side. What was he doing now?

I glanced over. Was he crazy enough to try scooting across to the next wall? If I remembered correctly, it was an easier top-roping one called the Mountaineer.

"Aaah!" I cried as I felt something smack me in the face. Something gooey and sort of slick. Gross!

I let go with one hand, swiping at the goop. Luckily it had mostly missed my eyes. I guessed it was the same stuff the guy had been dumping on the BMX track. He must've dumped it on me to slow me down.

A second later I realized it was even worse than that. He wasn't really aiming at me. He was pouring the greasy goop all over the wall itself! I could already feel my hand slipping. I grabbed for another handhold as my left foot skidded out of its hold.

"No!" I blurted out in a panic as I felt my right foot start to go.

I hugged the wall, clenching the handholds as hard as I could. But I could feel my entire body slipping on the goopy mess. How high up was I? A hundred feet, two hundred?

It was no use. I just couldn't hold on. One hand lost its grip, then the other, and I was falling . . . falling . . .

Running on Empty

I was almost to the far side of the mountain when I heard Frank let out a shout. A few seconds later there was a splash. It sounded loud in the hushed, darkened park. Then silence.

"Frank?" I murmured, skidding to a stop. My heart pounded as I realized what must have happened. Frank had fallen from the Summit. Had he caught up with the guy, tussled with him, lost his grip? Was he hurt? The vision of Smith lying lifeless on the concrete danced through my mind.

I turned, ready to race back to check on Frank. Just then I spotted some movement on the upper ski slopes. Spinning around, I was just in time to see the masked figure skid down one of the trails.

He abandoned the snowboard he'd been using at the bottom, leaping over the low fence at the base onto the roof of a souvenir stand.

"Hey!" I shouted. "Stop!"

He heard me and jumped down from the roof with a grunt. Then he took off in the opposite direction.

I stood there for a second, not sure what to do. My brother could be in trouble. *Big* trouble. Then again, he could be just fine, albeit a little wet. Either way, I really wanted to go back and check on him.

But I knew what *he* would want. He'd want me to continue the chase. Still not totally sure I was doing the right thing, I took off after the bad guy.

He had a head start. But he was also a lot slower than me. Soon I was catching up.

That was when he reached the edge of one of the big man-made lakes that dotted GX. There were a bunch of Jet Skis lined up at the edge of this one. The guy leaped onto the nearest Jet Ski, gunning it out into the open water.

I gritted my teeth. Okay, if he wanted to do this the hard way, I'd play. Jumping onto another Jet Ski, I took off after him.

The guy headed straight across the lake. He leaped off the Jet Ski just as it crashed into the far edge, taking off again on foot. As I did the same, I saw that he was heading for the motocross course.

"Yeah, make my day, buddy," I growled. If he thought he could outride me over a motocross course, he had another think coming.

The guy jumped on a bike. But instead of heading out onto the course, he spun around and roared out onto the main path. Even better. Street riding was what I did every day. There was no way he was going to lose me now!

I grabbed another bike and followed as he sped down the pathway and around a corner. The chase just got crazier from there. First the dude turned down this little gravel path between the space shuttle and the drag-racing track, almost spinning out. At the other end, he rode across the path and down the grassy bank of a picnic area. There was a small tumbling stream in the middle. For a second I thought that might stop him.

But no. He gunned the bike, aimed for a high spot, and jumped it! "Bring it on," I muttered, leaning over my handlebars and aiming for the same spot.

Whee! The jump was actually pretty fun. But there was no time to focus on that. I got him in my sights again and hit the gas.

He was already riding up the slope and out of the picnic area. After jumping the curb, he sped down the pathway.

Most of the lights were off, but there were still a few neon signs blinking away. One of them was the big one over the main arcade's vaulted entrance. My eyes widened as I saw the guy aim his bike directly at the arcade.

I didn't slow down. In fact, I accelerated a little as I rode up the ramp and right into the arcade.

Did I mention that place is amazing? It's got every game I've ever seen and then some. Right in the middle is this huge, glassed-in cube that sort of floats over the whole place, with a great view of all the action. There's also something called the Head-2-Head Arena, though its giant TV screens were dark at the moment.

But I barely saw any of that. For one thing, there wasn't much light. For another, I was focused on keeping my balance as the guy zigzagged through the place, zipping down one row of games and up another. If he wiped out, I totally had him!

The guy turned out to be pretty good. He rounded one last corner, making a quick turn around a car game based in a full-size Formula One car. Then he sped out the entrance on the other side.

One of the park's many skateboarding half-pipes lay right across the way. I winced as I realized the guy was aiming straight at it. Was he crazy? At the speed we were going, it would be almost impossible to control the bikes down that kind of drop.

But he didn't slow down. So neither did I. I saw him disappear over the edge and heard the roar of his bike's engine. I held on tight as my own bike reached the edge. My stomach seemed to drop out of my gut as I went down, down, down. The tires squealed and skidded as they finally met the smooth surface. The jolt bounced me off the seat a little, but I kept my cool—and my balance. At the bottom, the other guy turned sharply and was riding out that way. Whew! I hadn't been looking forward to trying to get my bike back up over the far edge. . . .

The side slope was relatively easy. But it still slowed me down a little. By the time I burst out of the half-pipe area, my quarry was halfway down the next pathway. I gunned it and followed.

Sparks flew from his tires as he swung around. Now he was aiming straight at the tracks of the Old Glory roller coaster. Huh? I couldn't believe my eyes. Okay, I already knew this guy was nuts— you had to be to do the things he'd done. But was he really crazy enough to try riding a motocross bike up a set of coaster tracks?

He might be, but I wasn't. I squealed to a stop in front of the lowest spot of the coaster's tracks.

Dropping my bike, I leaped for the edge and grabbed on. Soon I'd pulled myself up onto the tracks.

Up ahead, I could see that my quarry was already in trouble. *Big* trouble. The bike was bouncing all over the place. Its engine let out a terrible whine.

The guy shouted loudly as the bike tipped. A second later it crashed to the ground some twenty feet below.

"Whoa," I murmured. The guy had leaped off just in time. Now he was hanging on to the tracks with both hands, his legs dangling off the edge.

I moved as fast as I could, trying to get up there before he recovered. But before I reached him, he was on his feet again. He ran farther up, using his hands to help himself along as the slope steepened sharply.

Still, I could tell he was already slowing down. I put on a burst of speed. This time there was no way he could lose me! Soon I was within twenty feet of catching up, then ten.

He let out another loud shout as he reached the top of the hill. I glanced up and saw why. There was a roller coaster train stopped there, blocking the path! The guy jumped into the rear car and scrambled at the controls. He was obviously trying to get the thing started, or maybe just release the emergency brake. But he wasn't having any luck.

"Gotcha!" I crowed as I leaped into the car beside him.

The dude turned toward me with an angry growl. I gulped, suddenly realizing how much bigger he was than me. And that we were currently at least fifty feet in the air over solid concrete.

He grabbed me by the shoulders. Uh-oh . . .

"Wait!" I shouted as he gave me a shove. My rear end hit the edge of the car. One more push and that would be it. "Listen, man. You really don't want to do this!"

I felt the guy's hands tighten like a vise on my shoulders. I scrabbled for the edge of the car, even though I knew I'd never be able to hang on.

"No!" the dude exclaimed suddenly. He yanked me back into the car so hard I almost fell on him. "You're right. I can't do this!"

I was so surprised at still being alive that it took me a second to react. I just watched in amazement as the guy sort of crumpled down on the seat and dropped his head into his hands.

"Uh, wha—?" I stammered.

"I can't do it," the guy sobbed. "I won't let anyone else get killed. I'm turning myself in!"

I blinked. His voice sounded sort of familiar, though I couldn't place it at first.

Then he reached up and yanked off his ski mask. My eyes widened in amazement. "It's—it's you!" I blurted out.

With a Bang

quish, squish, squish . . .

My sneakers slapped wetly and rhythmically against the pavement as I ran. Falling into the wave pool hadn't exactly been fun. But it sure beat the alternative. As a bonus, it had rinsed away most of the gooey gunk that guy had dumped on me.

As soon as I'd swum to the edge and climbed out, I'd started heading off after Joe. But I hadn't gone far when I heard the roar of motors somewhere off to one side. I'd headed that way, but the engines had stopped. They'd started up again a few moments later, and once again I'd turned to follow. But whatever Joe and his quarry were riding—unless I missed my guess, it sounded like motorbikes—they were way too fast for me to keep up. All I could do was run in the direction of the noise, hoping Joe was on top of things.

Finally I'd heard the motors stop. I'd also heard an alarming crash a few seconds later. Uh-oh . . .

I was almost relieved when I heard Joe shout shortly after that. Hey, at least that meant he was alive! Still, he sounded kind of panicky. That couldn't be good. It takes a lot to panic Joe.

Putting on an extra burst of speed, I raced around a bend in the path and came within sight of the roller coaster Erica had taken us on the day before, Old Glory. We were close enough to the park's main walls for the security lights to illuminate things a little. That gave me a great view of Joe and someone else clambering down the tracks.

"Frank!" Joe cried as he spotted me. "You're okay!"

"You too." I glanced curiously at the other person, who had just jumped down. My eyes widened as I recognized him. "Wallace?" I exclaimed. "Uh, it is Wallace, right? You were the one who did all this?"

The security guard's pudgy face sort of crumpled. "It was me," he admitted breathlessly. "Sorry to put you guys through this. So you two must be the secret agents McKenzie brought in, huh? This whole time I thought that was just a rumor."

I briefly wondered who had spilled our secret and how many people knew. But I supposed it didn't really matter.

"So you were the one who tampered with all the rides and stuff?" I asked. "The motocross tire, the black ice . . ."

"The UTV," Joe added. "The mechanical bull. And, of course, the climbing wall that killed Mr. Smith."

"Yeah, that was all me." Wallace looked pained. "But you have to believe me—I didn't want anyone to die. I swear!" He dropped heavily onto a handy bench. "I didn't even think anyone would get really hurt."

"Oh yeah?" I challenged him. "You had to know Erica would get at least a little hurt when you tossed that rock at her."

"Huh? You mean the boss's daughter?" Now Wallace looked confused. "I didn't throw anything at Erica. I'd never do that. Maybe one of the others . . ."

Joe rolled his eyes. "Yeah, right. If you really didn't want anyone hurt, maybe you should've stuck to the graffiti and the e-mails."

"E-mails?" Once again Wallace looked perplexed. "What e-mails?"

"You know. Those lovely little threats from your alter ego, Skater Hater," Joe said.

Wallace shook his head. "Look, I'm confessing to the stuff I did," he said. "But I swear, I don't know what you're talking about."

Joe looked annoyed, but I was ready to change the subject. The local police could deal with dragging a full confession out of Wallace. In the meantime, I had another question.

"Why'd you do it?" I asked. "I mean, you work here. Why sabotage your place of employment?"

A stubborn look came over his face. "Look, are you guys cops, or what?" he said. "Aren't you supposed to read me my rights or something?"

"We're not cops," Joe said. "But I bet the real cops will be thrilled to read you your rights, especially when they hear you're responsible for Mr. Smith's death."

At that, Wallace's defiant expression crumpled once more into despair. He let out a sob, though he swallowed it quickly.

"You're right," he said. "I shouldn't protect him."

"Him?" I prompted.

"Uncle Frederick. This was all his idea."

"Uncle Frederick?" cried Joe. "Wait, you don't mean that old dude with the cane, do you?"

"W. Frederick Jackson," I said grimly. "Let me guess. The *W* stands for Wallace?"

"It's a family name," Wallace said with a sigh. "He's actually my great-uncle."

After that, he spilled his guts. It turned out that old man Jackson's family not only owned a lot of property in the islands, as we already knew. He had actually owned this very island until McKenzie came along. He'd refused to sell, so McKenzie had managed to have it taken from him through eminent domain for much less than market value. According to what Wallace claimed, there might have been some bribes and shady dealings involved, though he didn't seem to know any details.

In any case, Frederick had been furious with McKenzie. He'd planned to sell the extra land for much more money so he could pay off some medical debts. So he'd convinced Wallace to help him, promising to pay his great-nephew enough to open his own mechanic's shop if they were successful.

"At first it didn't seem like a big deal," Wallace told us with a heavy sigh. "He got me a job here at GX, and I was just supposed to sort of spy on things and report back. He made sure I was on duty the night he came out to spray paint that graffiti. Stuff like that."

"But then things got more serious?" I prompted.

"Uh-huh." Wallace swallowed hard. "I'm pretty good with mechanical stuff, so Uncle Frederick wanted me to mess with a few things. Like that UTV. And the mechanical bull. And that fake bomb. And the snowmobiles—"

"Hang on," Joe interrupted. "The snowmobiles?"

Wallace bit his lip. "Yeah, that hasn't, you know, happened yet. You might want to do something about it before tomorrow." He shrugged. "Anyway, none of it seemed like a big deal. But then people started to get hurt, and then Mr. Smith . . ." He trailed off with another sob.

Joe and I looked at each other. It was time to call in the police to take over. "Do you have your phone on you?" I asked him. "Mine got soaked."

Then I glanced at Wallace, hoping he wouldn't panic and run off. But he was still slumped on the bench. Maybe it was the dim light, but he definitely didn't look panicked. More like relieved. Somehow, I didn't think we'd have any trouble hanging on to him until the cops arrived.

By the next morning, it was all over. Wallace and his great-uncle were in jail. They still hadn't confessed to the rock throwing or the e-mails—in fact, Jackson claimed he didn't even own a computer. Still, they'd owned up to the more serious mischief, and that was enough for the police.

McKenzie was thrilled with the collar. He told us so for about the fifteenth time as we stood atop the little walkway directly over the main gate, looking down on the crowd of eager fans gathered outside. The protesters were still out there too—minus W. Frederick Jackson, of course. But they'd been shuffled off to the side by the people lined up to get inside. It was about nine thirty a.m. At ten the park would officially open to the public.

Most of the celebrities were up on the walkway with us. They wanted to have a good view of the fireworks that were supposed to go off as soon as the gates opened. I wasn't sure how exciting daytime fireworks would be, but McKenzie had assured us it would be an awesome display, with tons of colored smoke and other cool stuff.

So now we were just waiting for the last few minutes to tick down on the big clock down in the main square. Joe and I were standing in a little cluster with McKenzie, Delfina and the baby, Nick, and Erica.

"I'm glad I called in ATAC," McKenzie said, clapping me on the shoulder. "You guys know how to get things done! Thanks to you, that sorry pair will rot in jail for a good long while."

"Er, speaking of that, sir," I said. "Any chance you might take it easy on Wallace? I don't think he's a bad guy—he was just going along with his uncle."

McKenzie stared at me thoughtfully. "I'll take it under advisement," he said. "If you're willing to stand up for him, Frank, it's worth considering."

Nearby, Nick heard and rolled his eyes. "Oh, please," he muttered under his breath.

Meanwhile Erica moved closer, grabbing my arm and pressing herself against my side. For a second I was startled. Then I glanced over and saw Bret Johnston, the Mr. Nice Guyz singer, staring at us from nearby.

"You're so brave, Frank," she cooed at me, sounding way girlier than usual. I thought about pointing out that Joe had made the actual collar. But I kept quiet, figuring this was just part of her request for me to play boyfriend.

Just then Cody Zane loped over to join us, which meant we had to stop talking about the case. McKenzie had already warned us that he didn't want anyone to know. Maybe that meant bad publicity really wasn't just as good as good publicity.

Cody looked none the worse after his close call the day before. "Yo," he greeted us all before turning to Joe. "Listen, I'm totally bummed we never got to test out that motocross course. If there's time later, want to give it another shot?"

Joe grinned as goofily as if Cody had just asked him to the prom. "Sure thing," he said, trading a high five with the skateboarder. "This time maybe we'll even get bikes that stay in one piece!"

Both of them laughed at that. Then they sort of drifted away into the crowd, chatting about who knows what.

That left me feeling a little claustrophobic, stuck between McKenzie and his stepdaughter. Erica was still leaning into my side, even though Bret Johnston had disappeared.

A few other celebrities came over to talk to McKenzie. I stood there feeling kind of awkward, since Erica still wasn't letting go of me. What felt like hours passed like that, though it was only about fifteen minutes, according to the big clock. At that point McKenzie was still so busy schmoozing that Erica had to reach over and poke him on the arm when the clock hit ten o'clock.

"Hey," she said. "It's time."

McKenzie glanced up sharply, then chuckled

when he caught sight of the clock. "Oops," he said. "Okay, here we go. . . ."

He fished a remote control out of his pocket. Holding it up, he made a big show of pushing one of the buttons.

"Galaxy X is officially open!" he shouted as a bunch of cameras clicked and a cheer went up from the crowd below. A band started playing down in the square. The gates creaked open.

KA-BOOM!

An earsplitting explosion rocked the entire park, making Delfina scream and a few other people gasp or shout in surprise. I glanced up, expecting to see fireworks bursting overhead. Instead I saw that the top of Mount McKenzie had just blown sky-high in a huge, fiery explosion!

Meanwhile the crowd was pouring in, cheering and hooting and dancing around as they watched the top of the mountain crumble. Sparks rained down everywhere, drifting toward us on the breeze. Most of the spectators seemed to think it was all part of the show.

But one glance over at McKenzie told me otherwise. His face was a mask of fury.

"Was that, uh, planned, sir?" I asked him quietly.

"No," he spit out through tight lips. "Definitely

not. Why would I blow up the centerpiece of this place? If you knew how much it cost to build that mountain . . ."

Joe had already split off from the crowd and hurried over to rejoin us. He was just in time to hear what McKenzie said.

"Any chance it was a mishap with the fireworks?" he asked.

McKenzie shook his head. "They're being shot off from way over there across the powerboat lake—see?"

I glanced over and saw a flash of light speed upward and burst into a pinwheel of lights and smoke overhead. The crowd gasped and cheered again. An urgent beeping sound brought my attention back. It was McKenzie's PDA. He pulled it out and blanched as he glanced at it.

"What is it?" I asked.

Wordlessly, he held it out so I could see the text message blinking there: I WARNED U!

I stared at Joe. He stared back. I was pretty sure he was thinking the same thing I was. There was no way Wallace or his uncle could have sent that message from jail.

That could mean only one thing. Sk8rH8r was still out there.

My gaze slid back to the ruins of Mount McKenzie.

Another set of fireworks burst overhead, bringing more excited cheers from the crowd. The huge, innocent crowd.

It seemed this mission wasn't over yet. Not by a long shot.

THE END (for now . . .)

FRANKLIN W. DIXON

THE HARDY BOYS

Undercover Brothers®

INVESTIGATE THESE TWO ADVENTUROUS MYSTERY TRILOGIES WITH AGENTS FRANK AND JOE HARDY!

#22 Deprivation House

#23 House Arrest

#25 Double Trouble

#26 Double Down

#24 Murder House

#27 Double Deception

From Aladdin
Published by Simon & Schuster

Great middle-grade fiction from
ANDREW CLEMENTS,
master of the school story

"Few contemporary writers portray the public school world better than Clements."
—New York Times Book Review

From Aladdin
Published by Simon & Schuster